KT-232-704

“And what about you, Raina?

Don’t you need somebody as well?” Nolan asked. Raina blushed and looked down for a moment.

“I have JJ,” she said, her voice staunch. “He’s all I need.”

Nolan nodded and then stepped a little closer. “I’d really like to see you again.”

Raina’s breath caught in her throat.

“Nolan, I’m flattered. B-but I don’t date anymore. I’m sorry.”

“I understand,” Nolan said, his brown eyes gleaming under the street lamp. “But if you ever change your mind, make sure you let me know, okay?”

She was well-advised to steer completely clear of Nolan Dane. She’d only met him four days ago and he was already heating her blood. She couldn’t—no, shouldn’t—entertain the idea. And yet, she still found herself wishing she could say yes.

“How long are you prepared to wait?” Raina joked on a nervous laugh.

Nolan smiled and gave her a look that sent curls of delight all the way to her extremities.

“As long as it takes.”

* * *

Lone Star Holiday Proposal is part of
The Texas Cattleman’s Club:
Lies and Lullabies series—Baby secrets
and a scheming sheikh rock Royal, Texas

LONE STAR HOLIDAY PROPOSAL

BY

YVONNE LINDSAY

First published in Great Britain 2015
by Mills & Boon, an imprint of Harlequin (UK) Limited,
Eton House, 18-24 Paradise Road, Richmond, Surrey, TW9 1SR

Special thanks and acknowledgement are given to Yvonne Lindsay for her contribution to the Texas Cattleman's Club: Lies and Lullabies miniseries.

ISBN: 978-0-263-26066-3

Harlequin (UK) Limited's policy is to use papers that are natural, renewable and recyclable products and made from wood grown in sustainable forests. The logging and manufacturing processes conform to the legal environmental regulations of the country of origin.

Printed and bound in Great Britain
by CPI Antony Rowe, Chippenham, Wiltshire

A typical Piscean, *USA TODAY* bestselling author **Yvonne Lindsay** has always preferred her imagination to the real world. Married to her blind date hero and with two adult children, she spends her days crafting the stories of her heart, and in her spare time she can be found with her nose in a book reliving the power of love, or knitting socks and daydreaming. Contact her via her website: yvonnelindsay.com.

As always, I'm strengthened by the support of my fellow authors when working on a project like this, whether they are directly involved in the continuity or not. In particular I would like to dedicate this book to Soraya Lane to thank her for her constant cheerleading and encouragement, and for challenging me to bigger, better word counts than I ever dreamed I could achieve in a single day. Deadlines become so much easier when you're haranguing me from the sideline! Thank you.

One

Nolan rolled to a stop in the parking area at the Courtyard and looked around. The four-mile drive out of Royal had been pleasant, quite a difference from the Southern California freeway traffic that was a part of his daily grind back home.

Home. He grunted. Royal, Texas, was really his home, not the sparsely furnished luxury apartment he slept and occasionally ate in back in LA. But he hadn't lived here in Royal, or even been back, in coming up on seven years. Even now he'd chosen to check into a hotel rather than stay with his parents. The reminders of his old life and old hopes were still too fresh, too raw. He gave his head a slight shake, as if to jog his mind back on track, and pushed open the door to the brand-new SUV he'd hired for his visit. He alighted from the vehicle, grabbed his suit jacket from the backseat and pulled it on before taking a moment to adjust pristine white shirt cuffs.

The wind cut right through the finely woven wool of his

suit. It seemed even Armani couldn't protect you from a frigid Texan winter breeze. Nor were highly polished handmade shoes immune to the dust of the unsealed parking lot, he noted with a slight grimace of distaste. But when had he gotten so prissy? There'd been a time when even baby spit hadn't bothered him.

A shaft of pain lanced through him. It still hurt as if it was yesterday. Nolan buttoned his jacket and straightened his shoulders. He'd known coming back would be hard, that it might rip the scabs off wounds he'd thought already healed. But what he hadn't expected were these blindsiding moments when those old hurts threatened to drive him back down on his knees.

Pull it together, he willed silently, clenching his jaw tight. He'd lived through far worse than these random memories that were all that was left of his old life. He could live through this. It was time to harden back up and get to work.

As private attorney for Rafiq Bin Saleed, Nolan was here to do a job for one of Rafiq's companies, Samson Oil. He loved his work—particularly loved the cut and parry of entering into property negotiations on behalf of his boss and friend. The fact that doing so now brought him back to the scene of his deepest sorrow was tempered only by the fact that he also got to spend some time with his parents on their home turf. They weren't getting any younger and his dad was already making noises about retiring. From personal experience working there, Nolan knew that his dad's family law practice was demanding, but he couldn't quite reconcile himself to the fact that his dad was getting ready to scale down, or even walk away, from the practice he'd started only a few years out of law school.

Again Nolan reminded himself to get back on track. Obviously he'd have to work harder. Being back home after a long absence had a way of derailing a man when he least expected it—but that wouldn't earn him any bonuses when it came to crunch time with his boss. He looked around the area that had been christened the Courtyard. The name fit, he decided as he took in the assembly of renovated ranch buildings that housed a variety of stores and craftsmen. His research had already told him that the tenants specialized in arts and crafts with artisanal breads and cheeses also on sale, while the central area was converted into a farmer's market most Saturday mornings.

To Nolan's way of thinking, it was an innovative way to use an old run-down and unprofitable piece of land. So what the hell did Rafiq want with it? He knew for a fact that there was no oil to be found in the surrounding area. Hell, everyone who grew up in and around Royal knew that—which kind of raised questions as to what Samson Oil wanted the land for. So far, Rafiq's quest to buy up property in Royal failed to make economic sense to Nolan.

Sure, he was giving owners who were still battered and struggling to pull their lives together after the tornado a chance to get away and start a new life, but what did Rafe plan to do with all the land he'd acquired?

Nolan reminded himself it wasn't his place to ask questions but merely to carry out the brief, no matter how much of a waste of money it looked like to him. Rafiq had his reasons but he wasn't sharing them, and it had been made clear to Nolan that it was his place to see to the acquisition of specific parcels of land—whether they were for sale or not. And that's exactly what he was going to do.

Regrettably, however, it appeared that Winslow Properties, despite their shaky financial footing, were not open to selling this particular parcel of land. It was up to him to persuade them otherwise. He'd hoped some of the tenants would be more forthcoming about their landlord but so far, on his visits to the stores, he'd found them to be a closemouthed bunch. Maybe they were all just scared, he thought. Royal had been through a lot. No one wanted to rock the boat now.

There was one tenant he'd yet to have the opportunity to talk to. He recalled her name from his memory—Raina Patterson. From what he understood she might be closer to Mellie Winslow than some of the other tenants. Maybe Ms. Patterson could give him the angle he needed to pry this property from the Winslow family's grip.

He began to walk toward a large red barn at the bottom of the U-shape created by the buildings. The iron roof had been proudly painted with the Texas flag. The sight of that flag never failed to tug at him; as much as he'd assimilated to his California lifestyle, he'd always be Texan.

Looking around, Nolan understood why the Winslow family had, after initial interest in Samson Oil's offer, grown cagey at the idea of selling this little community and the land it was on. For a town that was still rebuilding, this was an area of optimism and growth. Selling out from underneath everyone was bound to create unrest and instability all over again. Not everyone here could just pick up and create a new life in a new town or state like he had.

Damn, and there he was again. Thinking of the past and of what he'd lost. His wife, his son. He should probably have sent someone else on the legal team to do this job but Rafiq had been adamant he handle it himself. He mentally shrugged. It was the price he paid for the obscenely high salary he earned—he could live with that as long as he didn't ever have to live here again, with his memories.

Raina made a final tweak of the pine boughs and tartan ribbons she'd used to decorate the antique mantelpiece and looked around her store with a sense of pride and wonder. *Her* store. Priceless by name and by nature. She'd been here in the renovated red barn a month now. She still couldn't quite believe that a year after the tornado that had leveled her original business and much of the town of Royal, she'd managed to rebuild her inventory and relocate her business rather than just fold up altogether.

It certainly hadn't been easy, she thought as she moved through the store and let her hand drift over the highly polished oak sewing table she'd picked up at an estate sale last week—but it had been worth it.

Now all she had to do was hold on to it. A ripple of disquiet trickled down her spine. Her landlord, Mellie Winslow, had been subdued yesterday when she'd visited Raina but had said she was doing everything she could to ensure that her father's company, Winslow Properties, didn't sell the Courtyard.

Raina needed to know this wasn't all going to be ripped away from her a second time. She didn't know if she had it in her to start over again. Losing her store on Main Street, and most of her underinsured inventory of antiques, had just about sent her packing from the town she'd adopted as her own four years ago. She had to make this work, for herself and for her little boy.

No matter which way she looked at it, though, she still couldn't understand why anyone would be interested in buying the dried-up and overused land, let alone an oil company. If only Samson Oil—who'd been buying land left, right and center around Royal—would go away and let her have the peace and security she'd been searching for her whole life. Heck, it wasn't even as if they seemed to be doing anything with the properties they'd bought up. At the rate Samson Oil was going, Royal would become a ghost town.

"Mommy! Look!"

Raina turned and smiled at her son, Justin, or JJ as he was known, as he proudly showed off the ice cream cone her dad—his namesake—had just bought him. JJ was three going on thirteen most of the time, but today he was home from day care because he'd been miserable with a persistent cold. He was back to being the little boy who wanted his mommy and his "G'anddad" most of all. The theory had been that he'd rest on the small cot she had in her office out back, but theory had been thrown to the wind when JJ had heard his beloved granddad arrive to help Raina move some of the heavier items in the store.

Looking at JJ now, she began to wonder if she'd been conned by the little rascal all along. The little boy had protested his granddad's departure most miserably, but he was all smiles now with an ice cream cone and the promise of a sleepover on the weekend.

"Lucky you," she answered squatting down to JJ's eye level. "Can I have some?"

JJ pulled the cone closer to him, distrust in his eyes. "No, Mommy. G'anddad said it mine."

Raina pouted. "Not even one little lick?"

She saw the indecision on his face for just a moment before he proffered the dripping cone in her direction. "One," he said very solemnly.

Raina licked off the drips before they hit the floor and theatrically sighed in pleasure. "That's so yummy. Can I have more?" she teased, reaching for JJ's wrist.

"No more, Mommy! Mine!" JJ squealed and turned and ran, laughing hysterically as Raina growled and lumbered playfully behind him.

Through her son's shrieks of delight, Raina heard the bell tinkle over the main door, signaling a potential customer.

"Justin Junior, you stop right there! No running through the store," she called out, but it was futile. JJ was barreling away from her at top speed.

She rounded the corner just in time to hear a muffled "oof!" as JJ ran straight into the man who'd just entered the store. The man was wearing a very expensive looking suit, which, she groaned inwardly, now wore a fair portion of JJ's ice cream cone, right at the level of the man's groin. JJ rapidly backed away. The stranger looked up, a startled expression on his face as his eyes met hers. A frisson of something she couldn't quite put her finger on ran between them like a live current. It unnerved her and made her voice sharp.

"JJ! Apologize to the gentleman, right now."

She couldn't help it—even though it was her fault for chasing him, she couldn't prevent the note of censure that filled her voice. And she still felt unsettled by that look she'd just exchanged with a total stranger. A look that left her feeling things she had no right to feel. Raina dragged her attention back to the disaster at hand and searched around for something to offer the man to help him clean up.

The only pieces of fabric she had close by were a set of handmade lace doilies from the early twentieth century. She certainly couldn't afford to lose inventory, but then again, nor could she afford to lose a potential customer either.

JJ turned his little face up to hers. His blue eyes, so like her own, filled with tears that began to spill down his still-chubby cheeks. His lower lip began to quiver. He dropped what was left of his cone on the floor and ran to her, burying his face in her maxi skirt as if he could make himself invisible.

"Hey, no harm done," the man said, his voice slightly gruff and at odds with his words.

Raina definitely noticed a hint of Texas drawl as she glanced from her son to the customer, who, despite that initial look of shock, now appeared unfazed by the incident. He reached into his suit pocket and pulled out an honest-to-God white handkerchief. Was that a monogram in the corner? Raina didn't think they had such things anymore.

"I'm so sorry, sir. Here, let me," she started, reaching for the cotton square.

"Might be best if I handle this myself," the man replied.

Oh, heavens, she was such an idiot. Of course he'd have to handle it himself. It was *his* groin, after all. She had no business touching any man's trousers, let alone there. She gently set JJ to one side and got busy picking up the cone that he'd dropped on the floor, gathering the sticky mess in her left hand.

"JJ, can you go fetch me the tea towel that's hanging up in the kitchen?" she asked her son. "And no running!"

It was too late. JJ raced away as if he couldn't wait to put distance between himself and the mess he'd created.

"Kids, huh?"

The stranger finally smiled and Raina looked up at him—really looked this time—and felt a punch of attraction all the way to the tips of her toes. Before she could answer, JJ was back and, ridiculously glad of the distraction, Raina used the cloth to wipe up the residue from the floor and then wrapped up the cone in the towel to deal with later. Her customer had likewise dealt with the mess on his trousers.

"See, all cleaned up," he said, rolling up the handkerchief and shoving it in his pocket again.

Raina cringed at the cost of getting all that fine tailoring back into pristine condition again. "But the stain. Please, let me get your suit dry cleaned for you."

"No, seriously, it's no bother. Is this your boy? JJ is it?"

She nodded and watched as the man squatted down so he was at eye level with JJ, who had cautiously turned his head around when he'd heard his name. She couldn't help but notice how the fabric of the stranger's trousers caught snugly across his thighs and, despite hastily averting her gaze, she also couldn't stop the disconcerting rush of acute feminine awareness that welled inside her.

"Hey, JJ, no harm done, except to your ice cream. I'm sorry about that, champ." When Raina started to protest that he had nothing to be sorry for, he merely put up one hand and kept his attention on her little boy. "Are you okay?"

JJ nodded.

"But you lost your ice cream. Maybe I can talk to your mommy about buying you another one. Would you like that?"

Again Raina went to protest but the man shot her a glance and a smile that made her hush. As embarrassed as she was by what had happened, she found herself prepared to follow his lead.

JJ nodded again and the man put out one hand. "Good," he said with another smile. "Sounds like we have a deal. You want to shake on that?"

Raina felt a tug of pride as her son extended his grubby little hand to be engulfed in the stranger's much larger one. But pride was soon overtaken by something else as she noticed the man's hands. They were tanned and broad, with long fingers and neatly kept nails. Definitely an office worker, she surmised, and not from around here, but—oh boy—there was that swell of attraction again. What on earth was wrong with her? After Jeb, she'd sworn off men. She couldn't trust her own judgment anymore.

The man rose to his full height, which dwarfed Raina's own five foot seven by a good several inches. He held out his hand toward her.

"Nolan Dane, pleased to meet you."

Automatically Raina took his hand but realized her mistake the moment she did so. A sharp tingle of electricity sizzled up her arm the second their palms met.

"I… I'm R-Raina. Raina Patterson."

She groaned inwardly. Great, now she sounded like a complete idiot. Her heart skittered in her chest as she noticed he was still holding her hand. She gently pulled free and fought the urge to rub her palm on the fabric of her skirt. “Welcome to my store, Priceless. Were you looking for something in particular? Perhaps I can help you,” she asked, forcing herself to put her business voice on.

His first reaction to her had been instant, visceral and totally unexpected. Now Nolan could barely tear his eyes from her. She looked so much like his dead wife, Carole, it was uncanny. Her shoulder-length hair was the same shade of glossy brown that hovered between dark chocolate and rich espresso. She had the same shape of chin and brows. But it was only once he looked more closely at her that he saw the differences that set them apart.

The woman before him now wore only a bare minimum of makeup, letting her natural beauty shine, whereas Carole had been so caught up in projecting the right appearance that even he had rarely seen her without makeup on. Even at breakfast. Carole’s argument had been that while he’d comfortably slipped into a law practice with his father, she’d had a harder road to travel, proving herself against the good ol’ boys in one of Maverick County’s corporate law firms. She’d needed all the armor she could get.

But there was something in the way that Ms. Patterson carried herself, too, and the sweetly serene smile she wore, that continued to remind him of his late wife. Raina presented a strong and untroubled facade to the world. A facade that he already knew hid a vulnerability that had been evident in her hesitant introduction and which had appealed to the protector in him with surprising force.

Hell no, he reminded himself forcibly. No matter how much she fascinated him, he absolutely couldn’t go there. Women like Raina Patterson were completely out of bounds. Even if she wasn’t married—which she probably was—she had a kid, and he had strict rules about not complicating his life any further. He'd already had his heart torn out and shredded to pieces once and he would bear those scars for the rest of his life. Dating was strictly for brief respites—and this woman did not look like the type for a quick roll in the sheets followed by an even quicker farewell.

"Thank you," he said, finally pulling himself together. "I just came to look around, to be honest. The Courtyard hasn't been operating long, has it?"

"No, not terribly long. It stopped being a working ranch a few years ago. The ongoing drought forced the original owners to sell and the new owners, the Winslows, came up with the idea to convert it to shops and studios. It's helped a lot of us get back on our feet after the tornado."

Nolan nodded as he processed the information and matched it up with what he knew already. "And you're selling antiques here?"

"Yes, and running craft classes out back. My first one is tonight. Would you be interested in signing on for a lesson in candle making? They're going to be a hot gift item for Christmas this year in Royal."

She laughed softly and, unexpectedly, he delighted in the sound. It was refreshing. Genuine amusement wasn't often heard in the circles in which he moved, at least not without some malice in it somewhere.

"I'll take a rain check," he said with a wink, and he was delighted to see a faint blush color her ivory cheeks.

"A shame," she said averting her head slightly. "I'm sure all the ladies would have been thrilled to have you."

And then he felt the heat of a blush on his cheeks, as well. Ridiculous, he thought. He hadn't blushed since the day he'd asked Carole out in high school and yet here he was with cheeks aflame. The memory was just the cold dose of reality he needed. It was time to get out of here before he made a complete fool of himself and broke his own rules about dating and asked the enticing Ms. Patterson out. He made a show of looking at his watch and made a sound of surprise.

"I need to get on my way, but first I should remedy the demise of JJ's ice cream."

"Oh, please don't worry. He'll be fine and, besides, the homemade ice cream store will be closed now."

"And I'm holding you up from closing, too, I see," he said, gesturing to the face of his watch. "I'll head off."

"Please, don't rush away. Look around—you never know—something might grab your attention. We'll be a little while closing up anyway."

Despite his determination to put some distance between them, Nolan found himself agreeing to prolong his visit.

"Okay, thanks. Let me know when you want me out of your way."

She nodded and gave him another of those serene smiles that delivered a solid whack to his solar plexus.

As he moved among the pieces she had on display, he reexamined his options. He was here to do a job. Part of that job was gathering information. He hadn't missed the spark of interest in her eyes. Perhaps he could use that interest to his advantage. Ms. Patterson, whether she knew it or not, had just become his best opportunity to get an angle on Winslow Properties and hopefully the leverage he'd need to pull off this purchase. Somehow, he needed to get past his emotional barriers and see her purely as a means to an end. If he didn't, all bets were likely off, and he'd have to deliver Rafiq his first failure in this acquisitions venture. Nolan's need to succeed pushed through. He could do this. And he would.

Nolan could hear Raina moving around toward the back of the store. He flicked a look her way and saw her laying out egg cartons and wicks and precut blocks of what he assumed was wax. JJ was doing his best to help. Raina moved quietly behind him and straightened up the things he laid out for her, and every now and then she paused to wipe his little nose.

She did everything with grace and an effortless elegance that mesmerized Nolan, and he had to force himself to look away and remind himself he was here to gather intel about the Courtyard, not spend his time mooning over one of the proprietors. He was on the verge of leaving the store when he overheard Raina talking to JJ.

"Well, how about that?" she said, putting her hands on her hips and looking around the workroom. "We're all done, JJ. I couldn't have done it all so fast without your help."

Nolan fought back a smile. He had no doubt she'd have had it done in half the time, but it tugged at his heart to see how she took the time to make JJ feel special and his efforts valued. Then came a fresh debilitating wave of sorrow as he remembered all he'd lost. Even so, he still couldn't tear himself away from the tableau in front of him.

"I'm a good boy, aren't I, Mommy?" JJ said, his little chest puffed out with pride.

"Yes you are. The very best. And you're all mine!" She reached out to tickle him and he giggled and squirmed out of reach. "How about, as a reward, I take you to the diner for dinner before your sitter comes tonight."

The little boy nodded vigorously. An idea occurred to Nolan. This was an opening he could use. He still owed JJ an ice cream. What better opportunity to fulfill his promise to the kid and to *accidentally* bump into his mother again and draw her back into conversation.

She'd mentioned a sitter. Did that mean there was no Mr. Patterson around? He gave himself another mental shake. Whether there was or not, it made no difference.

This would merely be another opportunity to ask her more questions about the Courtyard and Winslow Properties.

At least that's what he told himself.

Two

Raina heard her cell phone ring in her handbag as she was securing JJ in his car seat. Whoever it was would just have to leave a message, she thought as she did up his harness and checked to make sure he was snug. Finally satisfied, she got in the driver's seat and turned on the ignition.

"Seat belt, Mommy!"

She smiled at JJ in the rearview mirror. "Yes, sir!"

He giggled in response, the way he always did, and it made her heart glad. She thanked God every day for the gift of her son. Jeb Pickering might have been a useless no good son-of-a-bitch but he'd left her with a gift beyond price. While it would have been her ideal wish to have provided JJ with both a mommy and a daddy who loved him, she was happy to parent alone. In fact, given Jeb's reliability, or lack of it, and his predilection for gambling and drink, JJ was better off not knowing the man even existed. Of course, being a single mom running a business brought its own issues, including relying on sitters when her dad wasn't free to help out. Which reminded her—the phone call. Maybe it had been her sitter calling.

"I'm just going to check my phone, JJ, then we'll head to the diner, okay?"

"C'n I have nuggets 'n' fries?"

"You sure can."

"Yum!"

Satisfied that he could have his favorite meal, JJ hummed quietly to himself, kicking a beat on the back of the front passenger seat while he waited. Raina stifled the admonition that sprang to her lips when he started to kick. She didn't want to enter into an argument with him now. Instead, she reached into her bag and dragged out her phone. One missed call, unknown number. A sick feeling of dread crept into her gut. Quelling the sensation, she listened to the message.

"Hey Rai, it's Jeb. I hear you got your little shop up and running again. That's good, 'cause I'm in a bit of a bind. I really need some money, honey." He sniggered and Raina cringed. He sounded drunk, again. "Anyway, I owe some guys… I, uh, well, I'll tell you when I see you. Soon, babe. By the way, how's that kid of ours? Later!"

Raina deleted the message instantly, her skin crawling. She felt as if she needed a long hot shower. Hadn't it been enough that he'd emptied out her bank account and skipped town when she'd been at the hospital in labor with JJ? And what about the extra five grand she'd given him early last year for what she'd told him was absolutely and totally the last time ever?

"Mommy, I'm hungry!" JJ demanded from the back, his kicks picking up in tempo.

Raina reached across to still his little legs. "JJ, what's the rule about kicking in the car?"

His little mouth firmed in a stubborn line. *Pick your battles*, Raina reminded herself, morphing into distraction mode instead. "Are you having ketchup with your chicken nuggets?"

"Yay! Ketchup!"

"Let's go then," she said with a smile as she put the car into gear.

It was a short drive into Royal but traffic was heavy. Raina was lucky to get a parking spot on the road about a block away from the diner. JJ skipped and jumped, holding her hand, as they walked along the pavement. Judging by his energy levels, she hoped he'd be okay to go back to day care tomorrow.

When they entered the Royal Diner, JJ hopscotched along the black-and-white checkerboard linoleum floor. They took a booth near the back and settled in on the red faux-leather seats.

"Be with you soon, hon," a waitress said with a smile as she poured glasses of water and left them with the sheet menus that everyone knew by heart but still pretended to study anyway.

Raina's appetite was gone, but she decided on a green salad with ranch dressing because she knew if she didn't eat, she'd be running on empty by the time her craft class started in a couple of hours. Shoving all thoughts of her ex to the back of her mind, she focused instead on her son and the evening ahead.

All going well, JJ would eat his dinner and she'd take him home to shower before the sitter arrived. Once the sitter was there, she'd be able to head back to Priceless to open up for her first class. Bookings had initially been slow but they'd picked up in the past day or so, and she hoped the simple candle-making class would be well received and that word of mouth would bring more students. With more students would come more overhead but she'd done her homework. After the initial outlay was met, the classes would bring in more sorely needed income, as well.

A movement across the booth made her look up from the menu she was staring at but had stopped actually seeing several minutes earlier. JJ was waving at someone. Thinking it might be their waitress returning for their order, Raina looked up with a smile, only to feel it freeze on her face and the hairs at her nape prickle to attention as she recognized the man walking toward them. Nolan Dane. What was he doing here? Surely he was more likely to be dining out at the Texas Cattleman's Club, or at the hotel in town?

It took only a few seconds to notice that he'd changed. His jeans were new and fit him perfectly, and the black Henley he wore under a worn leather jacket seemed to stretch across his chest as if it caressed him. Her cheeks flamed at the thought.

"Mommy! Man!" JJ said from his booster seat, and he waved again.

"Hey there," Nolan said as he drew next to the table.

"I'm having nuggets 'n' fries," JJ informed him importantly. "You wanna eat with me?"

"Oh, no, JJ. I'm sure Mr. Dane has other plans," Raina said quickly, feeling her blush deepen on her cheeks.

"Please, call me Nolan and, actually, no, I don't. But I don't want to intrude. I can eat at another table."

Raina felt terrible. She'd all but told him he wasn't welcome to sit with them. JJ's face fell. How bad could it be? she asked herself.

"Oh, please sit down. Seriously, it's okay. We haven't ordered yet, anyway. Join us."

"Well, if you're sure."

She nodded and gestured to the empty space next to JJ's booster seat. Nolan slid into the booth and stretched his long legs out under the table. She shifted slightly as his leg brushed hers.

"Do you guys eat here often?" Nolan asked.

"No, this is a treat for JJ. Aside from the mess with your suit, he's been a really good boy for me today, haven't you, JJ?"

JJ nodded emphatically and reached for his water glass. Nolan helped him steady the large glass as he drank and then put it back on the table for him.

"You're good at that," Raina commented. "Do you have kids of your own?"

A bleak emptiness appeared in his eyes, its presence so brief she wondered if she'd imagined it, but it was enough to make her realize she'd been prying where she had no right to.

"Oh, I'm sorry. I shouldn't be so rude. I didn't mean to pry."

"No, it's okay," Nolan brushed off her concern. "Maybe we should just put it down to self-preservation. I've seen how lethal he is with an ice cream cone."

Nolan watched Raina from across the table and silently congratulated himself on managing to keep his past locked firmly where it belonged. The waitress came by and took their orders, distracting Raina from asking any further questions. She was less relaxed than she'd been when he'd left the store. Was it his presence at the table that did that to her, he wondered, or was it something else? The waitress returned promptly with JJ's order, and while the little boy dug in, Nolan thought it time to ease conversation back to the Courtyard.

"So tell me a little more about the Courtyard," he started.

"The idea for it really only took off a few months after the tornado. A lot of us lost our stores and several of Royal's local artisans lost workshops and homes. The Courtyard gave us all a fresh start—gave us a new community to be proud of." Her eyes grew worried and a frown marred the smoothness of her forehead. "There's talk that some oil company is looking to buy the land. It worries me."

"Why's that? What difference would a new landlord make?" Nolan probed.

Raina looked away, her face thoughtful, before directing her blue gaze straight back at him. "The Courtyard actually became a symbol of hope for a lot of us. A chance to get our feet back firmly on the ground and get us back to normal in a world that got turned upside down in one awful day. You can't put a price on that. We need stability now. We need to be able to know from one day to the next that after all our hard work, we aren't simply going to be turned out.

"An oil company isn't going to want to keep us as tenants, you can be sure of that. They'll want the land for testing, although why they think there's oil there, I don't know. I haven't lived in Royal all that long and even I know the land is barely suitable for grazing, although with the drought that's questionable, too."

She fiddled with the salt and pepper shakers in front of her. "No, the Winslows did the right thing turning the ranch buildings into the Courtyard. Mellie assures me they're not selling. I only hope nothing happens to change her mind. None of us there can afford to have our businesses fold or see our rents increase. What with the cost of increased insurance premiums and setting up all over again, it wouldn't take much to destroy us."

A pang of guilt pulled at him. If he was successful in changing the Winslows' minds, and Rafe got hold of the Courtyard, Nolan knew there were no guarantees that his boss would keep the tenants. And it was true. Raina had a point—while the greater Maverick County area had yielded some successful oil fields, none had been in this general area. Nolan shifted uncomfortably. For the first time he was seeing the personal face of his assignment:

someone who'd be directly and negatively impacted by his boss's plan. And he didn't like it. Not one bit.

He took a sip of his water and decided a change of subject might be in order.

"So, the tornado. That must have been terrifying. People are pretty resilient here, though," he commented.

Raina smiled and once again he was struck by how natural and effortless her beauty was.

"Sometimes I think Royal is the epitome of the 'get down and get on with it' ethic. Some people have moved on, which is completely understandable, but most have just licked their wounds and carried on. And of course there are also the lucky ones who are benefiting from the damage. Tradesmen have been at a premium in the district and we've seen an influx of out-of-towners coming in to fill demand. Bit by bit Royal has found its way back to a new normal. Is that what brings you here? The rebuild?"

Nolan was saved from immediately answering as their waitress dropped their meals in front of them with a smile. "Good to see you back, Nolan," she said before racing off to her next customer.

Raina looked taken aback. "You're local?"

"No, not anymore. I'm here to see family."

"You grew up here, then?"

He nodded. "Yeah, but I've been living in California for several years. I'm only here for a visit."

"Then I'm sure you would have heard all about the tornado from them." Raina's voice held a note of reserve that had been missing before.

"From their point of view, yeah. Dad's in family law, and he said he's seen an unfortunate upswing in business in the wake of the tornado. Families breaking up under the strain of trying to put their lives back together—more domestic abuse."

Raina nodded. "Yeah, it's sad. So often these events

pull people closer together, but if they don't they seem to have the complete opposite effect. I guess I'm lucky I didn't have to factor that in. It's just me and JJ, and my dad. Dad's retired and usually travels around the country, but he came to stay in the trailer park just out of town so he could be on hand to help me reestablish Priceless and get me and JJ back on our feet again."

Nolan couldn't help it: a swell of relief that there was no partner in Raina's life bloomed from deep inside. He pushed the sensation away. She was still out of bounds. She was the kind of woman who had long-term written all over her, while he was only planning to be here long enough to complete the land purchases to Rafiq's satisfaction.

And then there was the kid. He certainly didn't want to take on a package deal of mother and child, no matter how much his libido sizzled like a drop of water on a hot skillet whenever he was anywhere near Raina. He needed to keep his eye on the main goal. He was here to do business, not dally with the locals or become emotionally involved in the town he grew up in. He'd made his choice to walk away from Royal and all the pain it represented seven years ago. He had no plans to stick around. Even so, he perversely wanted to know more about the woman sitting opposite him.

"So, what brought *you* to Royal?" he asked.

She laughed, the sound self-deprecating. "I followed a man. He left and I stayed. It's as simple as that."

Somehow Nolan doubted that it was quite as straightforward as she said.

"Mommy, my hands dirty." JJ spoke up from beside him.

"Use your napkin, JJ."

"But it dirty," he grumbled.

"Here, use mine," Nolan offered.

JJ held his hands up for Nolan to wipe them. “P’ease?” he implored.

Nolan automatically enveloped JJ’s hands with the large paper napkin and made a game out of cleaning the little boy’s fingers. When he was done, he wiped a bit of sauce from JJ’s chin, as well.

“Hey, you’re good at that,” Raina said with a smile. “Are you sure you don’t have kids?”

Nolan swallowed. This would be the perfect opportunity to segue into the past, to admit he’d had a wife and child, but he couldn’t bring himself to say the words. It just opened up the floor for too many questions—questions that had no answers and only evoked pity, which he hated.

“Maybe I’m just a clean freak,” he joked, scrunching up the used napkin and tossing it on the table.

“Can we go now, Mommy?” JJ asked.

“No, son. Mr. Dane and I haven’t finished our meals.”

For a second it looked as though JJ would object, but then Nolan remembered his earlier promise.

“What about some ice cream? You never got to finish the one you had before, right?”

“Oh, but I said you didn’t need—” Raina began to protest.

“Need doesn’t enter into it when ice cream is concerned,” Nolan interrupted her smoothly. “What do you say, JJ? Do you want a junior sundae?”

“Wif sprinkles?”

“Sure, my treat.” He looked across at Raina. “How about you? Do you want a sundae with sprinkles, too?”

JJ laughed next to him. “Mommy doesn’t have treats, she’s a mommy!”

Nolan read the subtext in JJ’s words. It didn’t take a rocket scientist to figure out that Raina went without so that her son could have little treats every now and then. How much had she foregone to ensure her son could still enjoy special things while she rebuilt her business and kept a roof over their heads? Again that urge to protect swirled at the back of his mind.

"Even mommies like treats sometimes, don't they?" he asked, looking straight across the table at Raina.

"Not tonight, thank you. I need to get back to Priceless. My first class starts this evening and I can't be late, not even for a treat."

"Another time then," Nolan promised, and as he called the waitress to order JJ's sundae, he found himself wondering just how soon that might be.

Three

Another time? Did he mean to ask her out on a date? Raina wasn't quite sure how she felt about that. She hadn't dated since Jeb—hadn't even been interested in dating as she came to grips with his betrayal, single parenthood and running a business. It had been a painful irony that she'd been duped by the person she'd thought would stand by her, exactly as her father had been.

She had never known her mother and pictures of her had been few and of poor quality. Raina's enduring memory of the woman who'd borne her was the story of how she'd come home from the hospital with Raina, put her in her bassinet and gone out to buy some milk and never returned. Growing up, Raina had always had more questions about the whole situation than answers and, in retrospect, she could understand why she'd been drawn to the losers.

Despite all the security and love her father had poured into her, Raina's sense of self-worth had been low. She'd found herself desperate to be accepted by others, only to be walked all over again and again. Jeb had been the last in a string of disastrous relationships, and when he'd cleaned out her bank account while she was in labor with his son, she'd finally learned her lesson—and with it, who she was and where she belonged in her world. Now, she was at peace with her decision to focus her energies on JJ and provide a home for them. She finally, at the sage old age of thirty, felt grown up.

Her friends still teased her about her dating moratorium but she'd avoided all potential setups they'd thrown her way. And in the aftermath of the tornado, it had made far better sense not to get involved with anyone. Life had become incredibly precious and despite her need to nurture and to try to "fix" broken souls, aka the losers she'd dated previously, she'd had to draw a line somewhere.

But a date with Nolan Dane? He was nothing like the guys she'd been out with before. He owned a suit, for a start, and showed the kind of manners her father had always told her to expect from a man.

She looked across the table and noticed that JJ had made short work of his sundae and was now rubbing his eyes and fidgeting in his booster seat. She glanced at her watch—a 1920s timepiece she hadn't been able to bring herself to sell after she'd discovered it in a boxed lot she'd bought at an estate sale a couple of years ago. If she didn't get on her way soon, she'd be running late for the sitter and for her class.

"This has been lovely," she said, gathering her bag and searching for her wallet. "But JJ and I really must get going. Thank you for joining us."

"No, thank *you* for *your* company. Please, let me get this. It's the least I can do for crashing your dinner together."

"Oh, but—"

"Please, I appreciated having someone to talk to over my meal."

Before she could say anything, Nolan left several bills on the tabletop, including a generous tip, and helped JJ from the booth.

"Are you parked far away?" he asked as they walked toward the exit.

"No, not far. A block."

"Let me walk you," Nolan said, falling into step beside her on the sidewalk outside the diner.

"Mommy, up," JJ interrupted, and he lifted his little arms in the air.

"Sure, sweetie," she said, bending to lift him into her arms.

She wouldn't be able to keep this up for too much longer. JJ was getting so big and most of the time she had trouble keeping up with her energetic wee man. The fact that he wanted her to carry him spoke volumes about how tired he was. She reminded herself to cherish these moments while they lasted.

They were halfway down the block when she had to readjust JJ's weight in her arms.

"He looks heavy," Nolan commented. "Can I carry him for you?"

"No, it's fine, I can manage," Raina insisted, even though her back was starting to ache a little.

"Man carry me, Mommy."

JJ squirmed in her arms, almost sending her off balance.

"Are you sure you don't mind?" she asked Nolan.

In response, Nolan effortlessly hefted her son from her and propped JJ on one hip. "Of course not."

At the car, Nolan waited on the sidewalk while she strapped JJ into his seat.

"Thank you for dinner, and for your help with JJ. You didn't have to," Raina said as she straightened from the car and held her hand out to Nolan.

He took it and again she was surprised by the sizzling jolt of sensation that struck her as his hand clasped hers.

"Honestly, the pleasure was all mine," he replied, his eyes locked on hers.

She found herself strangely reluctant to let his hand go and Nolan seemed to feel the same way, but then a group of people coming along the sidewalk forced them apart. Thankful she could disengage before things got awkward, Raina gave him a small wave and settled herself in the car.

Her hand still tingled as she reached forward to put the key in the ignition. It had been a long time since she'd felt anything like this at a man's touch. As she drove away, Raina made herself keep her eyes on the road in front of her. She wouldn't look back. Looking back only invited trouble, she told herself, and she'd had bushels of that already in her life. No, she'd promised herself to keep moving forward the right way, and that didn't involve complicating her life with a relationship or fling with someone who was passing through.

Nolan watched from the sidewalk until he couldn't see Raina's taillights any longer. Why had he done this to himself? he wondered as he hunched deeper into his jacket and began to walk back to his hotel. Carrying JJ had brought back a wealth of hurt and repressed memories of his own son, Bennett.

Holding another small body in his arms…it had been a more bitter than sweet experience. He reminded himself very firmly that using her for information about the Winslows was one thing, but he was in no way embarking on any kind of friendship with Raina. It would be too easy, he knew that. He was already attracted to her, already felt that surge of physical awareness every time she smiled or her gaze met his. From the moment he'd laid eyes on her he'd been drawn to her and he'd been unable to get her out of his thoughts.

Being there in the Royal Diner with Raina and JJ had felt too much like his old life. The life he'd vowed he would never turn back to. No, his home was Los Angeles now. Royal held no allure for him anymore even though everything here still felt so achingly familiar.

He acknowledged the doorman at the hotel with a smile and went straight to his room. It was early. Any other time he'd have stopped in the bar and had a drink. Maybe enjoyed a bit of casual female interest before heading to his room—or hers. The mobile nature of his role as Rafiq's personal attorney gave him leeway in his life that he'd never allowed himself before and while casual hookups had never been his style, a man had needs—and clearly the women he'd met had needs, as well. But while those encounters may have left him physically sated, there always remained an emptiness deep inside him.

His thoughts flickered back to Raina Patterson. She was definitely not the type for a casual hookup. She exuded stability and comfort. A man could fool himself that he belonged in the softness of her arms, but only until he broke her heart by leaving again. Nolan promised himself he would not be that man.

He threw himself on the bed and reached for the TV remote. Maybe he'd be able to numb his mind and his awakened libido by watching some mindless sitcoms or movies until he was ready to sleep. But distraction was a long time coming that night, and he couldn't stop his mind wandering back toward the woman who'd so captured him.

Raina was glad she'd taken the time to prepare the workroom before she'd left Priceless earlier that day. JJ had been surprisingly clingy when she'd left him at home with the sitter, making her wonder if their company over dinner had unsettled him. It had certainly unsettled her.

Her students began to arrive, right on time, and once everyone was there and introductions were complete, Raina started the lesson. She'd decided to keep it simple for the first session, changing the style of the candles each week as they carried on. She smiled as she made eye contact with one of JJ's previous babysitters. Hadley Stratton was only a couple of years younger than Raina and had a delightful way with children.

"Okay, ladies, thank you all for coming along tonight. I see you all received my email with the instructions for preparing for this evening's lesson. Does anyone have any questions so far?"

Hadley spoke up. "You said we could dye the egg shells, but what if we could only get brown eggs?"

"No problem," Raina assured her. "You can choose to keep your candles in the shell and decorate the shells, or you can break the shell away after the candles have set and simply burn them in a container—like an eggcup or something like that. It's entirely up to you."

"I'm so brain dead after nannying all day and studying all night that I think I can only go as far as filling a shell. Is that okay?" Hadley laughed. "Maybe I can leave decorating to another lesson."

Several other women joined in with Hadley's laughter, obviously empathizing with her. Raina nodded in acknowledgment.

"How many of you would prefer to decorate or color?"

About half the women in the room put their hands up.

"Okay," Raina said. "How about we split into two groups for tonight? Decorators this side of the workroom, and plain beeswax candles on the other."

The women good-naturedly shifted around and, after showing the group doing plain candles how to start the process of melting their beeswax, Raina discussed with the group of decorators how to dye their egg shells or hand paint them with freestyle or stenciled designs. As everyone set to work, Raina began to feel a sense of excitement. The lesson was really going well and the atmosphere was both lighthearted and creative at the same time.

She stopped by Hadley's table for a minute, while making the rounds of the class to check that everyone was on track.

"It's good to see you, Hadley. We miss you."

"I miss you guys, too. But you know what it's like balancing everything."

"You always make everything look so effortless when you're with kids. You should really have some of your own one day," Raina teased with a friendly smile.

Hadley laughed out loud, drawing attention and several smiles from the people around her. "I've got so much on my plate right now I'm quite happy to put that off for a while longer. Besides, there's the important prerequisite of finding the right man for the job, y'know?"

Raina felt her smile slip a little, but she knew Hadley hadn't meant anything by her comment, that she hadn't been referring to Raina's poor choice of partner in Jeb.

"You make sure he's the right one, then," Raina said, with a light touch on Hadley's arm.

"Don't you worry, I will. When the time is right. In the meantime, at least I have your classes to look forward to on Tuesday evenings. This is about as far as my social life extends. Getting to spend time with other adults and relax and unwind is like gold to me right now, plus I get to make some cute Christmas gifts at the same time. What more could a woman want?"

With a murmur of agreement, Raina moved on to her next student. Hadley was right. What more could a woman want than to be surrounded by people she enjoyed being with and doing something creative? Even so, Raina felt an unexpected yearning that pulled from deep inside. She wanted that "right one" in her life one day. The man who would be her partner in everything and help her to guide JJ on his path in life. Right now, while JJ was small and so dependent on her, it was easy to imagine that she'd be able to cope forever. But sometimes she wished for more. For herself, as well.

Nolan Dane popped immediately to mind and Raina quashed a startling swell of desire as adequately as she was able. This was ridiculous. She'd only met the man today and she was already spinning a tale of happy ever after in her mind? Clearly she wasn't busy enough with her life already. Pushing all thoughts of men to the back of her mind, she went to assist one of her students with the placement of her candle wicks.

By the time the class finished, everyone was proud of their results—Raina most of all. Not only had she successfully pulled off tutoring her first official craft lesson, but everyone had commented how much they were looking forward to returning the following week when they'd be making mason jar candles filled with oil. Some were even talking about classes in the New Year and how they'd like to bring other friends along.

When everyone had cleaned up and gone, and Raina had locked up, she drove herself home. After paying the sitter and checking on JJ, she decided to run herself a luxurious deep bath. She'd earned the hot soak, she decided as she stripped and pulled on a robe while waiting for the bath to fill. In fact, she'd earned a celebratory glass of wine to go along with it. After a quick trip to the kitchen she was soon back with a glass of merlot. She disrobed and lowered herself into the soothing water.

Everything was going to be okay, she told herself. While the antiques business was a little slow in getting off the ground again, she knew it wouldn't take too long before her old customers would discover her new location. A bit of careful advertising across the county would help, and now, with the popularity of the craft classes, as well, she could afford to place those advertisements. She took a sip of her wine and allowed the mellow flavors to roll across her tongue before she swallowed.

Yes, everything would be fine from now on. She and JJ wouldn't want for anything. Or anyone.

Later, as she readied for bed, she checked her phone for messages. She'd turned it off during her class and hadn't gotten around to turning it back on yet. A bit of the shine of happiness from the evening's success dulled when she saw she had another missed call from Jeb and that he'd left another message. Her finger hovered over the button to simply delete the message, but she couldn't bring herself to do it. Instead, she listened and felt her happiness dull a little more.

"Rai, c'mon, babe. Call me back. I really need some money fast. I know you're good for it. Look, this is pretty urgent. Call me."

Raina closed her eyes in frustration. When would she ever be rid of the man? She'd taken all the legal steps she could to have sole custody of JJ, so she knew the little guy was safe from his father. But what would it take for Jeb to leave her alone?

Stop giving him money. The words echoed in her head as clearly as the last time her father had uttered them to her. Not for the first time she wondered why she continued to help her ex. It wasn't because she still bore any love for him. That had died long ago. Was it because she felt beholden to him because of JJ? No. She'd made the decision to go ahead with raising him, knowing it was unlikely that Jeb would provide any support. Maybe it was just because, despite herself, she couldn't help but reach out when she knew a man was down. Her father had often teased her about her need to make everyone happy and feel safe. The thing was, if she kept helping Jeb, when would he ever learn to stand on his own feet and accept some responsibility for everything that happened in his life?

She came to a decision. This ended here and now. She'd no longer be Jeb's cash cow or his go-to person. She deleted the message and shoved her phone in her purse and climbed into bed. Let that be an end to it, she thought as she closed her eyes and drifted off to sleep.

Four

Nolan strolled around the Courtyard the next afternoon, telling himself he wasn't there to see Raina Patterson at all, he was merely doing his job and finding out a bit more about the other tenants. If he could present the acquisition of this parcel of land to Rafiq as an ongoing business concern rather than merely as a land purchase, maybe he could preserve the jobs and incomes of these hardworking people.

He was taken by the work in the silversmith's shop. The delicacy of the silversmith's designs was exquisite and Nolan knew his mother would love the pendant designed to look like a peacock tail with tiny cabochon amethysts and peridots inset at the ends of the feathers. He eyed the price tag and decided that the cost didn't matter. His mother's pleasure on opening the gift would bring its own reward. She'd had little enough joy from him in the past few years as he'd avoided returning to Royal. Maybe this would help show her that despite his withdrawal from home, she was still very much in his thoughts.

The shop assistant was effusive about his choice, almost talking him into purchasing a matching set of earrings, but he knew that less was very definitely more when it came to his mother's tastes and that she preferred a few well-chosen pieces to a cacophony of color and design.

"Is this a Christmas gift?" the woman asked.

"No, just something my mom will enjoy," he answered.

"Ah, that's lovely. Would you still like me to gift wrap it for you?"

"Please."

"Are you new to the area?" the assistant asked as she deftly wrapped the pendant in tissue and wrapping paper.

"I grew up here but I've been away for a while. Just here to see my family."

"Oh, that's lovely," the woman said with a friendly smile. She tied off a length of organza ribbon around the little packet and popped it in a gift bag. "Well, thank you for supporting the Courtyard with your purchase. I hope we see you back before you head home."

Murmuring a note of assent, Nolan took the gift and left the store. It was only midweek but the parking lot was almost full of vehicles and people were bustling around, their arms filled with bags emblazoned with the local artisans' logos. This place really was a gold mine. Yesterday he hadn't spent enough time wandering about, getting a real feel for the place—it was something he was determined to remedy today.

A flash of color caught his eye and he turned his head to see Raina Patterson outside her store, assisting a customer putting a small side table in the back of their car. He felt a now-familiar wallop of awareness as he took in the way her bright red sweater dress clung to her feminine curves and skimmed her hips like a lover's caress.

His body heated and sprang to life, arousal beating a low thrumming pulse that reminded him all too much of the dreams he'd endured last night.

Dreams where he'd begun to make love to his late wife, but when she'd turned toward him it had been Raina's face before him instead.

Nolan swiftly veered into the nearest store, determined to bring his body back under control and rid himself of the desire to walk those few yards toward the big red barn and spend time again with its proprietor. He wasn't here to embark on an affair, he reminded himself. He was here to work.

Raina looked up, surprised to see Nolan Dane on the other side of the Courtyard. She raised a hand to wave, but it appeared that he hadn't seen her as he abruptly turned and headed into the cheese maker's store. She told herself it didn't matter, that she hadn't hoped to see him again anyway. Even so, she felt a tiny twinge of disappointment that she forced herself to rapidly shove aside. She had enough on her plate for today as it was. The class she had lined up for tonight was mosaic work, and she had yet to check the inventory of stock she'd ordered for her students to buy and use for their lessons. The simple mirror frame kits would hopefully be a quick and easy project for her students to tackle, all of them first-timers to mosaic work, and she was looking forward to the class.

A prickle of uneasiness ran down her spine—the sense of disquiet making her look around before heading back into the store. She must be imagining things, she thought, pushing the feeling away and delving into the boxes of stock she'd left on the workroom tables. Last night's message from Jeb was making her paranoid and goodness knew she had little enough time for that.

* * *

The week went quickly and her classes were going from strength to strength. As a side bonus, several of her students were also avid collectors of a variety of antique items including some of the delicate English china she had on display. She was excited to have sold several pieces already and had requests to look out for more. Things were going better than she'd anticipated.

By the time Friday night rolled around, she was really beginning to feel the strain of carrying the responsibility of the store and the classes on her own, and she wanted nothing more than to sit at home with JJ, tucked up in front of the fire and reading a few of his favorite storybooks. But she'd already promised him that they'd go downtown to the Christmas tree lighting ceremony organized by the Texas Cattleman's Club. It was her goal to one day be sponsored to join the club. Of course, she'd need to make a better than average income before she could afford to do that.

While the club had been a solely male domain when it was founded, in recent years women had become members and the club had become more family-oriented in general. And they did such good work in the community, too. Something she hoped to be able to participate in when the time was right. It was important to give back.

The evening air was cold and Raina made sure JJ was bundled up snug and warm in a jacket and hand-knitted wool beanie that one of her customers had made for him. He looked as cute as a button with a few dark tufts of hair poking out from beneath the beanie.

She helped him from the car when they got to downtown Royal, and for a second she felt a pang of regret that Jeb couldn't be a part of JJ's life. But JJ deserved a father he could rely on. Not one who drank and gambled and drifted from one town to the next, looking for work to support his habits.

She'd been blind to Jeb's faults for a long time and forgiven him time and again, believing his well-spun lies, right up until the day he wasn't there when she needed him most. JJ's birth had been a roller coaster of emotions: intense joy to finally hold her child in her arms and meet him face-to-face that was tempered by the realization that the only people Raina could honestly rely upon were herself and her dad. She'd grown up a heck of a lot that day. She'd thought herself so mature at twenty-seven, so ready to be a mother.

"Will there be gifts under the tree, Mommy?" JJ asked as he skipped along beside her on the sidewalk, holding her hand.

"Not real ones, my boy."

"Not even one for me?"

Raina laughed and tugged his beanie more securely over his little ears. "Not even for me either! But don't worry. I'm sure that Santa will remember exactly where we live and will bring you your gifts in time for Christmas."

Satisfied with her answer, JJ turned his attention to the growing crowd. In the distance, Raina caught sight of Clare Connelly. The chief pediatric nurse at Royal Memorial Hospital had been a wonderful support when JJ had been severely jaundiced after his birth and Raina had worried herself sick over him. Newly abandoned by her partner and with her father still on his way to Royal, Raina had had a severe dose of the baby blues as she began to doubt her ability to look after her newborn son. It had been Clare's confident and capable manner with the babies in her care, not to mention the gentle support she'd offered to the new mothers, that had made Raina begin to believe she could do this parenting thing all on her own.

Raina caught Clare's eye and waved a hello. Clare was involved in what appeared to be a very intense conversation with one of the pediatricians who'd also attended JJ at the hospital, Dr. Parker Reese. Raina raised her eyebrows in surprise. Was there something going on between the petite blonde nurse and the sometimes prickly pediatrician? The thought brought a smile to her lips. It had been a joke among the mothers in the hospital that Dr. Reese would make a great husband for someone one day—if he could ever let go of his work and develop a social life. The man was dedicated to his career but everyone needed some balance in their life.

The reminder of balance prodded at Raina's thoughts. Lately everything had been JJ and work for her. There'd been no time for herself, but she was okay with that. One day, maybe, when JJ was a bit older and when her business was on a stronger footing, then yeah, she might think about dating. Until then, she had to stay focused on keeping her financial footing and being the best mother she could be for her little boy.

"Mommy, I can't see," JJ complained, tugging at her arm. "Up?"

"Sure, baby."

Raina bent and lifted JJ into her arms, settling him on one hip. It probably didn't make a world of difference to his line of sight but it was all she could manage.

"Still can't see," he fretted, twisting in her arms and making her clutch his jacket to stop him from falling.

"JJ, settle down. Trust me, when the lights go on, you'll see everything."

"Here" came a familiar male voice. "Maybe I can help?"

"Man!"

JJ flung his arms toward the newcomer with an exuberance that dismayed Raina and almost sent her off balance. Nolan Dane loomed up beside her. She should refuse his offer of help, but JJ was already transferring himself into Nolan's arms and was soon deposited high on Nolan's shoulders.

"Better now?" Nolan asked, looking up at JJ who was holding on tight to Nolan's head.

JJ nodded.

"What do you say, JJ?" Raina prompted.

"T'ank you."

"You're welcome." Nolan turned his smile to Raina. "I hope you don't mind. You look tired and I could see he was getting heavy."

Raina's lips twisted into a smile. "It's okay, thank you."

So, he thought she looked tired, huh? Wow, way to build a girl up, she thought, then immediately chastised herself for being so churlish. She did look tired. The three late nights this week with the classes, on top of everything else, had taken a toll. She made a mental note to try to get to bed earlier on the nights she wasn't working.

The crowd around them thickened as the local singers and dance groups performed on the makeshift stage that had been set up for the evening. Raina's gratitude to Nolan for taking JJ increased. There was no way JJ would have seen the show, or enjoyed it, from her arms; nor would she have been able to hold him for this long.

The night sky was fully dark and the atmosphere quickly became one of excitement as, over the loudspeakers, the master of ceremonies and the newest Texas Cattleman's Club president, Case Baxter, led the countdown to the lighting of the tree. Everyone in the crowd counted with him.

"… Three, two, one!" Raina shouted along with the rest of the crowd, then she joined them in the oohs and ahhs of delight as the switch was thrown to bring a multitude of colored lights to life in the massive tree that now dominated downtown Royal. Tearing her eyes from the tree, Raina looked up at her son, whose face was a picture of enchantment. A deep sense of contentment filled her.

She might not own the world, but it sure felt like it when she could still put a look like that on her little boy's face.

A choir began to sing "Joy to the World," and bit by bit the crowd joined them. Nolan had a surprisingly pleasant tenor, Raina discovered as he unselfconsciously added his voice to the singing. As the song wound to its end, the mayor of Royal took the microphone and thanked Case Baxter and the Texas Cattleman's Club committee for sponsoring the tree lighting ceremony, and he concluded by wishing everyone the very best for the season and inviting them to support the retailers who'd set up stalls around the square.

Raina turned to Nolan. "Thank you. I really mean it. I'm sure he'll remember tonight for a long time to come and that's because you helped us out."

"Only too happy to oblige y'all," Nolan answered. "Say, do you have to race home right away? How about a churro and some hot chocolate from one of the stalls over there?"

"Yummy, churro!" JJ crowed from on top of Nolan's shoulders.

"Manners, JJ!" Raina admonished. "What have I told you?"

"T'ank you, man," JJ dutifully responded.

Nolan laughed and Raina felt her heart skip a happy beat at the sound.

"His name is Mr. Dane, not man, JJ," Raina gently admonished.

"I think you should let him call me Nolan. Mr. Dane sounds so stuffy."

Raina nodded her head. "I'll try but I can't guarantee it. He can be pretty stubborn when he decides on a word."

Through the crowd, she spied Liam Wade. The rancher was clearly in demand with the ladies and looking none too thrilled about the prospect. A group of very determined looking mommas with single daughters in tow had circled him like a wagon train, ensuring he had no easy way out. A chuckle escaped her lips, prompting a question from Nolan.

"What's so funny?"

"Oh, just poor Liam. He's one of Royal's most eligible bachelors," she said, pointing him out in the crowd, "and one of Royal's most reluctant at the same time. I think he'd be happy if he never had to leave his ranch."

Nolan chuckled in sympathy. "Yeah, I guess when you have an operation like the Wade Ranch you're pretty self-contained. I can see why he wouldn't want to leave, especially if he gets mobbed whenever he sets foot outside his property line."

"Sure, but everybody needs somebody, don't they?" Raina countered without thinking.

Raina caught Nolan looking at her—a strange expression on his face as if he was weighing her words. Did he need somebody? His eyes lingered on her mouth and she fought not to lick her lips in nervous reaction. But it made her wonder: What would his lips feel like on her own? She immediately shoved the thought away. Here he was with her son on his shoulders and she was thinking about him kissing her? What was wrong with her?

Nolan shifted his gaze. "And what about you? Don't you need somebody, as well?" he asked.

She felt color flood her cheeks. "I have JJ," she said, her voice staunch. "He's all I need."

Nolan made an indeterminate sound and guided Raina toward one of the stalls off to the side. He swung JJ down to the ground and rolled his shoulders a few times before marching up to the counter and placing an order. Had she upset him by saying that JJ was all she needed? It was hard to tell. And besides, she reminded herself, it shouldn't bother her if it had upset him. She wasn't in the market for a relationship. Even so, it didn't stop her watching him as he picked up the tray with their hot chocolate and churros and led them over to a seating area that had been set up to one side.

"Don't let it all get cold," he warned gently as he set the tray down on the table in front of them.

"Thank you so much for this," Raina said, transferring some of JJ's hot chocolate to a sippy cup she'd pulled from her bag. "Sorry, I just like to be on the safe side with drinks when we're out. I know he's probably old enough to do without—"

"Hey, no need to apologize," Nolan interrupted. "You're his mom, you know what's best for him. I'm hardly in a position to judge."

By the time they'd finished their treats, JJ was getting cranky and tired. There was no way he'd make the trek back to where Raina had parked so when Nolan offered to carry him for her again, she didn't object. Weariness pulled at her, too, but the thought of curling up in her bed was tempered by the need to get up early the next morning. Saturdays she opened late, because they were her yard- and estate-sale mornings when she rose before dawn to try to pick up the occasional treasure to resell at Priceless. Her dad always came over super early to take care of JJ for the day so she could go straight to the store after doing her rounds of the sales.

At the car, Nolan stood to one side while she settled JJ into his car seat. Poor kid, he was almost asleep already, she noticed. Straightening from the car, she closed JJ's door gently and turned to Nolan.

"Thank you so much for your help tonight. I really do appreciate it."

"I enjoyed it. It's always fun seeing the lights through a child's eyes. Kids make everything so simple, so basic and enjoyable, don't they?"

Raina smiled at him, then struggled to stifle a yawn. "Oh, my. I'm sorry. Please excuse me. It's been a heck of a week. I'd better head off and get JJ into bed."

Nolan nodded and then stepped a little closer. "Raina, I'd really like to see you again. To take you out to dinner or the movies?"

Raina's breath caught in her throat. He was asking her for a date? For the briefest of moments she cherished the idea but then her practical nature set in. She shook her head gently.

"Nolan, I'm flattered. Truly I am. But I don't date. My life is too busy as it is. It's really not a good time for me to be thinking about stretching myself any thinner. I'm sorry."

"No, it's okay," Nolan said, his brown eyes gleaming under the streetlamp. He reached into his back pocket and pulled out a card holder. "I'm disappointed but I understand. If you ever change your mind, make sure you let me know, okay? My private number is on the back."

He slid one pristine white business card from the holder and pressed it into her hand. The instant he touched her, that familiar tingle came back, except this time it quivered through her veins along with something else. Something that felt curiously like desire.

She held on to the feeling for the briefest moment, wondering when had been the last time anyone had made her feel like a desirable woman, before ruthlessly quelling it again. She couldn't—no, shouldn't—entertain the idea. It was best that she didn't see Nolan again. Every relationship she'd ever had had extracted a price whereby she'd lost a little bit of herself in the process. She daren't do that to herself, or to JJ, again. Not now. Not ever. And yet she still found herself wishing she could say yes.

"How long are you prepared to wait?" Raina joked with a nervous laugh, unable to stop herself from asking the question even though she had no intention of taking Nolan up on it.

"As long as it takes," Nolan said with a slow smile that sent curls of delight all the way to her extremities.

Oh, yes. She was well-advised to steer completely clear of Nolan Dane. She'd only met him four days ago and he was already heating her blood.

Unable to think of a suitable response, Raina muttered a swift good-night and got into the car. She gave Nolan a small wave as she pulled away from the curb and drove away. A red light at the intersection halted her retreat and she glanced in the rearview mirror. Nolan still stood there on the sidewalk, his hands shoved in his jacket pockets, watching them go.

She couldn't stop thinking of him during the journey home to their little rented house and, even after she'd put JJ to bed and found refuge between her own sheets, Nolan Dane remained front and center in her thoughts. The way he looked at her made her feel like a woman. Not just a mom, not just a retailer or a tutor, but a warm, desirable and wanted woman. She'd pushed the idea away so hard and so vehemently after Jeb that it had become a concept she'd almost forgotten. Seeing that attraction reflected in Nolan's face empowered her. It was a sensation she liked.

She twisted in her sheets, her body aching with unexpected longing. Nolan Dane affected her in ways she hadn't wanted to acknowledge but now that she'd opened the door on those feelings, they'd all come rushing out. She liked everything about him so far—his manners, his careful way of speaking, even the tone of his voice. And his eye-catching looks didn't hurt either. He carried his height with confidence, with his broad shoulders set straight, and he met a person's gaze square on with no subterfuge—no lies. Having been on the receiving end of those looks Raina had come to realize that a woman could get happily lost in those deep brown eyes of his.

And then there was his manner with JJ. Even at the store, on the first day she'd met him, he'd been so good with her little boy—so understanding after the disaster with the ice cream. Nolan was an out-and-out gentleman, there was no denying it. And he treated her like a lady. Going out on a date with him would be something special. Suddenly Raina was swamped with regret that she'd said no to his invitation. She shifted in the bed again and thumped her pillow into shape. If only she could as easily reshape her life, she thought as she settled back down.

Nolan was the last thing on her mind as she drifted off to sleep. Nolan, and the knowledge that the next time he asked her out, *if* he asked her out again, she might even say yes. After all, what harm could it do?

Five

Nolan walked back to his hotel rather than grab a cab. He was filled with an energy that demanded release—although walking wasn't the first activity that sprang to his mind. No, his mind was filled with the image of a certain dark-haired, blue-eyed storekeeper who had somehow inveigled her way into his thoughts and lodged there like a burr under a saddle.

He could still see the flare of awareness that had dilated her pupils when they'd touched only a short while ago. Hell, he could still feel it within himself. The only other person he'd ever felt that way about had been Carole. The reminder was a daunting one, and it should serve as a reminder that Raina Patterson was not the kind of woman he needed in his life. He'd been there and done that. He'd lived and loved within a perfect marriage with his perfect woman and they'd had the perfect little family—until it all fell apart.

Nolan went to step off the curb and was jolted into awareness by the blast of a car horn. Damn, he needed to keep his wits about him and Raina had managed to scatter said wits to the four corners of the earth. She was definitely not what he was looking for. He didn't even know why he'd asked her out, except that, for all his mental flagellation, deep down he still wanted her.

He nodded to the doorman as he entered the hotel and headed for the elevators. The sounds of music, conversation and laughter echoed across the marble-floored lobby from inside the hotel bar, catching his interest. He looked at his watch. It certainly wasn't too early to return to his suite but he was sick of his own company right now. Perhaps a distraction could be found elsewhere—one that would hopefully erase or at least dull the throb of desire Raina had left him with.

At the bar he ordered a brandy. It wasn't long before he had company. A blonde woman took the stool next to his and cast him a smile. He reacted in kind automatically and waited for the flicker of heat that usually signified an initial burst of interest. As they embarked on conversation there was no mistaking her interest in him, and yet he couldn't seem to kindle an answering response in himself.

Instead, before he'd even finished his brandy, Nolan excused himself and went up to his suite. And as he lay staring at the dark sky through his open bedroom windows over an hour later, he wondered if sleep was as distant for Raina as it was for him. He forced his eyes closed, but even then all he could see were still shots of her beautiful face—sometimes smiling, sometimes pensive.

Nolan reached into his memory for the sense of loss he'd carried with him since losing Bennett and Carole, but it was further away than it had been before. Instead, he found his thoughts drawn to another woman, one whose gentle personality and sensual warmth somehow had begun to fill a hole inside him he didn't even want to acknowledge that he had.

It was late when Nolan finally rose the next morning. As he shaved, he considered his next step. He'd always prided himself on being a man of action. It was what had gotten him through the bleak empty horror of the death of his son soon followed by that of his beloved wife. And if something was worth doing, it was worth doing well. He also had never been one to take no for an answer.

As soon as he'd finished getting ready and had enjoyed a late breakfast in the coffee shop next door to the hotel, he was in his rental and heading out to the Courtyard. He didn't even bother trying to mentally dress this visit up as being in the course of his work.

Fact-finding mission be damned. He'd had a niggling feeling that Raina was merely going through the motions when she'd turned down his invitation to a date yesterday. The words had fallen all too easily from those sexy lips of hers. As if she'd trotted the phrases out often enough for them to become automatic. That left him with two options. The first was to find out if she really meant what she said and the second, to discover what it was that she'd left unsaid.

As he drove out to the Courtyard, he considered his strategy for getting the truth out of Raina. Sure, he could go in and ask her straight out but he had a feeling that the shield she'd built around her was pretty darn strong and could withstand anything he could metaphorically throw at her. No, he'd go gently, softly. Try to understand where she was coming from and why she was so adamant about not dating.

He shook his head. Why was he even bothering? It wasn't as if he planned on hanging around after he'd finished his job for Rafiq. There'd be more dragons to slay back in Los Angeles, or maybe even somewhere else.

A smoldering ember of desire sparked deep inside him. That's why he was bothering. He wanted Raina. It was as impure and as complicated as that. He smiled a little at his twist on the old saying of things being pure and simple. Given that what his boss planned for Royal could mean eviction for Raina's store, Nolan should stay well back. But he couldn't.

He had to at least try with her, didn't he? Maybe it was a just physical thing, something he needed to get out of his system. But maybe it was something more.

As soon as he gave the thought a moment in his mind, its tendrils secured themselves as tightly as a stubbornly clinging vine. The analytical side of him demanded that he define what that "something more" could be, especially when he'd spent the past seven years telling himself he wasn't interested in long-term ever again. He'd lived the life he'd always dreamed of right up until the day it had turned into a nightmare his family had never recovered from. He owed it to them, to their memory, to keep what they'd had sacred. To keep it in the forefront of his thoughts so that he never let down another person or another family like that again.

He totally understood the pain that had driven Carole to take her own life. After all, didn't he choose to live with it every day and face it like the demon it was?

All of which brought him back to why he was so persistent about seeing the delightfully warm and sensual Ms. Patterson. Even he knew this attraction was more than a simple itch to be scratched. One look at Raina and he'd seen complicated all the way.

Before he realized it, Nolan was parked in front of Priceless. Through the windows he could see Raina moving about inside. His gut clenched on a swell of need that took him completely unawares.

He wasn't a man who'd ever taken rejection well, and that was probably what made him so good at his job. If one method failed, then there was always another, and another. Strategy, for him, was all about finding the weak points, then mercilessly exploiting them. His lips pulled into a wry grin. Wow, like that sounded sexy and irresistible. What woman could refuse an approach like that?

He was still smiling as he pushed open the door to the store and heard the chime of the bell above announcing his arrival. Raina lifted her head with a smile on her face to welcome him. Her smile froze for a moment, her blue eyes wide and vulnerable, before she composed herself and straightened from her task to greet him.

"Good morning. What brings you here today?" she asked, setting down the cloth she'd been using to polish the top of a box she was cradling in her other arm.

In pristine condition, the box housed a fountain pen with nibs and a crystal inkwell with an engraved silver lid. It was a beautiful set and, by the look of it, had barely been used. She left the lid open to better display its contents and set the case down on a nearby table.

"Christmas shopping," he improvised, moving closer to take another look at the writing set. "For my mother. I was hoping you'd be able to help me. Say, that looks interesting."

Was it his imagination or did her pupils dilate a little as he stepped closer? Raina had her hair pulled back into a ponytail today. The style exposed the delicate curve of her neck and the soft line of her jaw. What he wouldn't do to be able to take his time and lay a line of sweet kisses along those very contours, and more.

She took a half step back. "It's a writing set, from the

1920s, I think, judging from the art deco design on the pen."

"It's beautiful," he said, tracing the engraved pattern on the silver with a fingertip. He wondered what sort of price tag she had on the set.

"I recognize that look in your eye," Raina said on a short laugh.

"Look?"

"Of longing. I feel that way with pretty much everything in my store. Regrettably, I can't keep it all. Are you looking for something like this for your mom? It's a bit masculine. Or does your mother collect anything in particular?"

"Egg cups," he said abruptly after racking his brain and coming up with the first thing he could remember. "She loves English china egg cups."

Raina's smile returned. "Oh, then you're in luck. I have a few you can choose from."

She gestured for him to follow her across the broad plank flooring of the store toward a glass-fronted display cabinet. Selecting a key from the chain she kept hooked at the waistband of her jeans, she opened the cabinet and pointed out the exquisite pieces.

"These two are English. One Staffordshire, which as you can see comes with a salt pot and pepper shaker in the stand, and the other is Royal Winton, hazel pattern, with the toast rack, as well. This one here, though, is French."

She pointed to a delicately patterned gold-edged porcelain tray with six matching egg cups arrayed around a carry handle in the shape of a porcelain chick.

"Good grief," Nolan exclaimed. "And people use these?"

"Well, given their age it's safe to say people more likely used these in the past, while they collect and display them now. Would you like me to lift them out so you can take a closer look?"

Nolan nodded and bent to peer at them when Raina put

them on top of a nearby sideboard. As he studied them, Raina gave him a little commentary.

"The Staffordshire piece certainly looks the more sturdy, doesn't it?" she asked. "This one is from the nineteenth century."

"So old?"

She laughed. "Well, this is an antiques store."

He found himself smiling back at her and this time there was no mistaking the dilation of her pupils or the slight blush of pink on her cheeks as they made eye contact. She was attracted to him, he knew it as well as he knew the face that greeted him in the mirror every time he shaved.

"Good point," he conceded as she briskly looked away. "Which one is your favorite?"

She hesitated a moment before speaking. "While the Staffordshire is an exceptional example, with no chips or cracks, and the Royal Winton is also, I prefer the whimsy of the French pieces. Yes, they're a little more worn, but that comes with use and for me, use brings character to a piece. I like to imagine the family who might have enjoyed these egg cups, the children who might have touched the chick coming out of its china eggshell as they enjoyed their breakfast."

She gave an embarrassed laugh. "But then, that's me. And you said your mom collects English china, didn't you?

He nodded. "Maybe it's time she diversified across the channel to France, as well."

He studied the pieces again and then gave a decisive nod. "The French one it is."

"Nolan, you didn't even ask me how much it is!"

He shrugged. "Does it matter? It's for my mom. She'll love it, and probably for the exact same reasons you do."

Raina nodded in acceptance and then carefully put the other two breakfast sets back in the cabinet.

"Would you like me to gift wrap it for you?" she asked, carrying the tray to the counter.

"Please. And double the bubble wrap for me, would you? I'm terrified that I'll break it before I give it to her."

Raina eyed him teasingly. "You don't strike me as a careless man."

"Accidents happen," he said without thinking, his voice sharper than he intended. He knew that for a truth…all too well.

"Bubble wrap it is then. Plus I think I have a box out back that would be perfect. Would that suit you?" she said, picking up on his change in mood and making her tone more businesslike than before.

"Thank you," he replied, determined to inject more warmth into his voice. "I really appreciate it. Mom will be thrilled, I'm sure."

"I'm glad. It's always nice to know things will continue to be appreciated when they leave here. I kind of feel like a custodian for them, you know. Like I have a responsibility to the original craftsmen and -women to see that their hard work continues to be loved as it changes hands."

Her words summed her up perfectly, he thought. She cared about things and about people. So why then did she keep herself so aloof? It was time to find out.

"I imagine that you don't get a lot of time to yourself," he said leaning against the scarred countertop that looked as if it had seen many years of service somewhere in its life. "What with the store and JJ and all."

She kept her head bent and her attention on her task but he saw the slight change in her posture. As if she was shoring up her defenses.

"I get enough. In fact I get most Saturday evenings to myself when my dad is in Royal and takes JJ for a sleepover. That is plenty for me. I wouldn't change anything in my life for something as ephemeral as time alone and definitely not at the expense of my son."

"You sound like a woman who knows her own mind."

"I like to think so. Now, at least. I wasn't always this certain, but I guess when you've learned the hard way, you tend to take things a little more seriously."

"The hard way?"

Raina finished wrapping his mother's gift and swiftly tied a cheerful Christmas bow around the wrapping paper. "There you are. All done. Now, will that be cash or credit?"

She was avoiding answering him. That much was clear. He slid his platinum card from his card holder and passed it to her before placing both hands on the countertop and leaning toward her.

"Raina, I meant what I said last night. I really would like to see you, to get to know you better."

She looked up at him, a little flustered and a lot startled. He realized how much he was encroaching on her space and straightened up from the counter again.

"I… I told you last night, Nolan. I don't date. I just don't have time."

"What are you afraid of, hmm?" he coaxed.

Her eyes shone with what he suspected—hell, *hoped*—was yearning. He pressed forward with what he saw as his advantage.

"At least tell me why. You can't let me go away with a complex. Just think of what that could do to a man like me."

His deliberate foolishness earned its own reward when she laughed, openly and honestly and from the heart.

"Oh, I think your ego is completely safe from me," she said, passing back his card. "But if you really must know, I haven't exactly had the best taste in men. Take JJ's father for example. I met him near where we lived, over in the next county. He swept me off my feet and dazzled me with his grand plans. We moved to Royal when he got work here as a ranch hand, but he never quite seemed to be able to hold down a job for more than a few months at a time. Then he left me broke after cleaning out my bank account. I promised myself, there and then, that no man would ever leave me that vulnerable again."

Nolan sensed there was a great deal more behind her words than she was letting on.

"You never pressed charges?"

"He's JJ's father. Of course I didn't. I just hoped that he'd taken enough money that he'd never need to come back. But—" she cut herself off abruptly and seemed to gather her thoughts back together "—but that's all in the past," she said with false brightness.

Nolan could read between the lines and he knew there was much more to her story than the potted history she'd just given him. But it could wait. Instead, he latched on to something she'd said a few minutes ago. "You mentioned your dad has JJ on Saturdays?"

She nodded slowly.

"Today?"

She nodded again. Nolan felt a glow of excitement light up in his chest.

"So, if I asked you if you could break your no-dating rule and have dinner with me tonight, could I persuade you to consider it?"

Raina pursed her lips and crossed her arms but even though her body language was all about the "no," the yearning he'd seen in her eyes before was still very much in evidence. He held his breath while she took her time making her decision.

"Okay," she said on what sounded like a long held sigh. "Yes, I'd like that. But just dinner."

He smiled and fought the urge to fist pump the air in delight.

"Just dinner," he agreed. "Where and when can I pick you up?"

Raina gave him her address and they agreed on the time he would pick her up. He knew the area. Not the worst in town, but not the best either. Still, after what she, and the rest of Royal, had been through just over a year ago, at least she and JJ had a secure roof over their heads.

He could do so much better for her. The thought hit him from nowhere and left him reeling. He pushed it back. Looking after Raina Patterson wasn't his business; she'd made that abundantly clear. She was a strong and independent woman.

Which only made her all the more appealing.

Six

Nolan pulled up outside the address Raina had given him. The area was worse than Nolan remembered and he hit the automatic lock on his car key as he got out and walked up the path toward the house. Raina answered the door before he'd so much as lifted his finger to the doorbell. As excited to see him as he was to see her, perhaps? He certainly hoped so.

He let his gaze roam her body. She looked beautiful. Her silky dark brown hair shone loose and long as it fell about her shoulders, and she'd done some incredible magic with eye makeup that made her blue eyes even brighter and more intense than he'd ever seen them. There was a faint hint of blush on her cheeks and her lips had a delicious watermelon-colored sheen. He ached to lean forward and see if those lips tasted as good as they looked.

She wore a long sheer burgundy blouse, with a matching camisole beneath it, over slim-fitting black pants and high heels. A fine gold chain graced her neck and small pear shaped gold drops hung from her ears.

"I'm so sorry," she started, and for a second he thought she was going to pull out of their date. But then she said, "Dad dropped JJ back home earlier. He has a leak in the trailer right where JJ's bed is and since he had JJ with him all day he didn't get a chance to repair it. When I told him I'd planned to go out he said he'd be back to sit for me, but he's not here yet."

Nolan felt himself relax. Waiting for her father to return was no problem.

"That's okay. We have plenty of time," he assured her.

"Man!" JJ slid to a halt on the polished wooden floor in front of him.

"JJ!" Raina admonished. "His name is Nolan, not man."

"No'an." JJ tried the name out for size, then reached for Nolan's hand. "Come see Spider-Man."

Nolan looked to Raina for approval. She shrugged. "If you don't mind?" she said helplessly. "He's certainly fixated on you. Dad said all he talked about today was 'man' and the Christmas tree."

"I don't mind," Nolan assured her before looking down at JJ's eager face. "C'mon then, JJ. Show me Spider-Man."

The sensation of the little boy's fingers so trustingly wrapped within his own somewhat soothed the ache Nolan felt in his heart. Bennett had been only eighteen months old when he'd died. Less than half JJ's age. Would he, too, have been a fan of comic-book heroes? Nolan would never know.

JJ's excited chatter yanked him back into the present and Nolan fell into an easy banter with the garrulous child. Sure, JJ still struggled with some syllables but his overall command of language made him easy to understand as he bounced around his room in excitement—dragging one thing and then another from his shelves and drawers to show Nolan.

Down the hallway, Nolan heard sounds of another person arriving. A man with a deep voice. When he got to JJ's room, Nolan took him for Raina's dad immediately. He had the same piercing blue eyes and that determined set of the jaw. Raina stood behind him, looking a little uncomfortable.

Nolan rapidly got to his feet and extended a hand to the newcomer.

"Nolan Dane, pleased to meet you."

"Justin Patterson. Can I have a word with you before you leave with my daughter?"

The man's eyebrows pulled into a straight line and the no-nonsense look in his eyes set Nolan back a bit. He hadn't seen a look like that in a father's eyes since he dated back in high school—and he hadn't missed the proprietary use of the word *my* when referring to Raina either.

"Sure," he answered smoothly. "Just let me help JJ put his things back."

"I can do that," Raina said, stepping into the room. "You go talk with Dad, then we can leave for the restaurant."

"I'll only need a minute," her father said dourly from the doorway.

Justin Patterson didn't take long to get to the point. The moment they were out of earshot of JJ's bedroom, he bluntly told Nolan exactly what he expected.

"Treat my daughter with respect."

"You have no worries on that score, sir. Raina is a wonderful woman."

"I don't know what your intentions are toward her, but I will tell you this. If you break her heart, or if you hurt her in any way, I will come after you."

Raina's dad was Nolan's equal in height and had at least twenty pounds on him. He had the look of a man used to hard work and Nolan had no doubt that he meant every word.

"Thank you for being honest with me. Now let me be honest with you. I know Raina doesn't normally date, and we haven't even known each other very long, but I have no plans to hurt her. We're going out for dinner tonight, and that's all."

"Humph." The older man crossed his arms over his chest. "Make sure that *is* all you do."

Nolan understood where Justin Patterson was coming from, especially based on what Raina had said to him earlier. "I'm not in town for long and I respect your daughter too much to try to take advantage of her—although you misjudge her if you think she'd let me. So far, I think it's safe to say that we like each other and I enjoy her company. JJ's, too. Raina is safe with me."

Justin narrowed his eyes at Nolan. "Dane, you said. Your father is Howard Dane?"

Nolan nodded. His father was well known in Royal and his family law practice was well respected.

"He's a good man. Let's hope the acorn didn't fall far from the tree."

With that, Justin turned and went into the kitchen where Nolan could hear him bustling around and putting the teakettle on. Raina came into the room with JJ trailing behind.

"Go see what Grandpa is up to, JJ," she urged. "Maybe he's making hot chocolate for bedtime."

As the little boy scampered toward the kitchen, she looked at Nolan with an apologetic expression on her face.

"I'm sorry about that. He's kind of protective."

Nolan put up a hand. "No problem. He's your dad. He's entitled to be protective of you. So, are we okay? Shall we go?"

She nodded and called out, "We're on our way, Dad. Call me if you need me!"

Judging by Justin's grunt they were free to go.

Nolan helped Raina into her coat and held the front door for her as they went outside. Streetlamps shone like golden orbs in the air, casting light onto the road beneath them. He guided her to his SUV and closed the passenger door for her once she was settled.

As he climbed into his seat, Nolan saw a furtive movement near a bush a few yards away. His eyes strained to see what it was but it appeared there was nothing there. He shrugged it off as something he'd either imagined or perhaps an animal that was now long gone. But as he began to drive down the street, he caught a glimpse of a man briskly walking down the sidewalk.

There was something about the way the man carried himself and how he kept to the shadows that made Nolan's instincts go on alert. As they cruised by in the SUV, the man furtively kept his face averted and hunched his shoulders. Sure, it was cold tonight—certainly too cold to be out casually walking anyway—which could explain the man's posture, but even if he was out for a constitutional stroll, why was he doing his best not to be recognized? In his work Nolan had seen a lot of characters and to him it was clear that this guy didn't want to be noticed.

Nolan didn't want to alert Raina to his concerns. She was busy looking out the window at the other side of the road and therefore oblivious to what he had seen, but he remained uneasy. Had the guy been watching Raina?

The idea plagued him during the drive to the restaurant, even while Raina kept up a patter of general conversation, asking him about growing up in Royal. By the time they were seated and perusing their menus, Nolan had decided to put thoughts of the walker, whoever he was, from his mind. He was here to enjoy Raina's company and he didn't want anything to detract from that.

Later, when they were about to make their selections

for dessert, his cell phone began buzzing persistently in his pocket.

"I'm sorry," he said, sliding the device out to see who the caller was. Rafiq. Damn. His boss was hardly the kind of person he could hold a conversation with in front of Raina. "Will you excuse me a moment? I really need to take this call."

"No problem." She waved him on with a smile. "I need some time to decide on dessert anyway."

He excused himself and, lifting the phone to his ear, he answered the call.

"Rafe, what can I do for you?"

"You can tell me how things are going with the Courtyard acquisition for a start," his boss said without preamble.

"The Winslow woman is very resistant to selling."

"The Winslow woman? What happened to Homer Winslow?"

"He has been removed by his board for mismanagement," Nolan said, summarizing how Melanie Winslow had wrested control. He strongly suspected the proposed buyout of the Courtyard had been the catalyst for that. "Ms. Winslow now heads Winslow Properties."

"But she's a maid, isn't she?"

Nolan fought back a smile. Rafiq was very modern and forward thinking in many ways, but in others he was still a throwback to his family's roots in ancient Al Qunfudhah, on the coast of the Red Sea.

"Ms. Winslow has a very successful business providing house-cleaning and house-sitting services. She is quite a bit more than a maid, and she is proving to be adamantly opposed to the sale of the Courtyard."

"Offer her more."

"Are you sure you want to do that? When word gets around, and it will in a place like Royal, any other owners of property you're interested in will simply increase their asking prices accordingly."

Rafe made a sound of annoyance and Nolan could just imagine the expression on his boss's face.

"They still owe money on that land, don't they? Can we get any leverage through their lenders?"

"It's an avenue I'm looking into now. Rest assured. If we can buy the Courtyard, it will most certainly be yours."

"There is no 'if,' Nolan. I want that land."

Not for the first time, Nolan started to bite his tongue against the question of why Rafiq was so adamant about his acquisitions around Royal. To hell with it, he decided. He wanted to know and, as Rafe's agent in all of this, he damn well deserved to know.

"Why, Rafe? What's so important about that or any other piece of land you're buying?"

"My reasons are my own. Do not overstep the bounds of our friendship, Nolan. I'll be in Holloway next weekend. We will meet Saturday at 10:00 a.m. at the Holloway Inn."

It was just like Rafiq to make a demand rather than a suggestion. But Nolan was well used to his boss's manner.

"I'll be there."

"Good. I expect to hear more progress has been made on the situation then."

With that closing statement, his boss ended the call. Rafiq hadn't said as much but the implication was clear in his tone. Friendship or no, if Nolan wasn't happy to continue to act for him, there were plenty of other lawyers who would. He slid his phone back into his pocket and returned to the table.

Raina looked up as Nolan approached.

"Everything okay?" she asked, as he settled back down into his chair. "Was that work?"

"What makes you ask?" he said, evading her question.

"Probably that frown you've got right now."

He forced himself to relax and smile. "Better?"

"Much. Seriously though, is everything okay?"

"Sure, nothing that can't wait until tomorrow anyway."

He picked up his dessert menu and briefly scanned the contents without even really seeing them. Rafe's unwavering determination to purchase the Courtyard and the barren acreage it sat on didn't sit comfortably with him at all. In fact the whole business was beginning to leave a bad taste in his mouth. Sure, Royal had changed a lot since the tornado. It certainly wasn't the town he'd grown up in anymore, nor was it the one he'd left seven years ago. But deep down, the values and the lifestyles remained the same. What kind of impact would Rafe's plan have on all of that?

And what of the traders, like Raina, who'd picked their lives back up after total devastation and who needed the stability and continuity the Courtyard provided? Did Rafe plan to continue to run it as it currently operated, or did he plan to scuttle everything? There were just so many questions buzzing around like angry bees in Nolan's brain right now. It made it hard to recapture the pleasure he'd felt in Raina's company only a few minutes ago.

It was clear her trust in him was growing and he appreciated that far more than he'd believed possible. But by acting for Rafe, he was betraying that trust and he didn't like it.

"What have you decided on?" Raina prompted from the other side of the table.

"What are you having?" he countered.

"It was a tough decision to make," she said with a short laugh. "But I think I'll go for the white chocolate cheesecake."

He closed his menu card and laid it back on the table. "Same for me."

By unspoken mutual consent, they lingered over their coffees and dessert. Nolan didn't want to break the fragile spell that had rewoven itself around their evening by drawing things to a close, but when he caught Raina stifling another yawn, he knew it was time to take her home. Despite Rafiq's interruption, Nolan had thoroughly enjoyed the evening. And he knew without a doubt that he wanted to get to know Raina better.

Their drive back to her house was done in a companionable silence and, once they got there, Nolan walked Raina up the path to her front door. Haloed by the porch light, she looked like a beautiful angel but his thoughts and intentions toward her were anything but angelic.

"Thank you for this evening," Raina said. "I'd forgotten how much I enjoy adult conversation and company that's not related to kids or work."

There was a smile on her face that was wistful and it sent a pang to Nolan's chest. He could imagine she had little enough time to herself, let alone to share with another person.

"It was absolutely my pleasure."

Afterward he couldn't be certain who had made the first move. But it didn't matter one bit. His senses filled with her—her scent, her taste, the feel of her in his arms and, above all else, the beauty of her kiss. A sense of rightness filled him as their lips met, as his hand lifted to thread through her hair and to cup the back of her head. Inside him a knot began to unravel and he knew, in that moment, that he wanted Raina in his life. That he could finally begin to let go of the pain of the past that had kept him in emotional isolation.

He traced the softness of her lips with his tongue as they parted beneath him. Desire unfurled through his body, doubling on itself until it consumed his thoughts. When Raina's hands pushed through his hair and held him to her, he knew she felt the same. She pressed her body against his and heat flared between them.

Nolan deepened their kiss. His tongue probed her mouth and she responded in kind. A shudder of need pummeled him and he felt an echoing tremor from her.

Overhead the light flicked off and then on again.

He felt Raina pull away. Her lips were swollen and curved into a grin.

"I can't believe this. My father is obviously letting me know it's time for me to come inside." She gave a half-embarrassed giggle before leaning forward to kiss Nolan sweetly, and all too swiftly, on his lips. "I'm sorry. I'd better go in before he comes out with a shotgun."

"You're kidding about the shotgun, right?"

"Of course I am, but he's very protective. Thank you again, Nolan. For everything."

"We'll see each other again," he stated firmly.

"Yes, I'd like that."

"Soon."

She nodded and laughed, her breath leaving a misty cloud in the air between them. "Yes, soon. How about Monday night? Dinner here, with JJ and me."

"I'd really like that," Nolan said. Even though every minute he'd spent with JJ so far reminded him all too much of all the things he'd missed out on with his own son, he enjoyed the little guy's company and his simple enthusiasm for life. It was a poignant reminder that he needed to inject some of that enthusiasm back into his own. And maybe, just maybe, he needed to consider telling Raina about the wife and son he'd lost, too. "Monday, then."

"Is six o'clock okay with you?"

"Perfect. I'll be there. Can I bring anything?"

"Just yourself is fine. See you then."

She turned, put her key in the lock and opened the front door. Then, with a small wave, she was gone from sight. Nolan shoved his hands in his pockets and jogged down the path to his car. He drove back to the hotel, his mind only half on what he was doing while the other half raced ahead and churned over a million different thoughts.

Sleep would be a long time coming tonight. He hadn't expected anything like this when he'd returned to Royal. Hadn't wanted it. He'd been meticulous about his relationships in the past and particularly about avoiding any emotional entanglements. But somehow this attraction had found him and lodged itself within the gaping hole of loneliness he had come to accept as being as much a part of him as every breath he took.

And it felt good. In fact, it felt better than good—it had brought back to life something he hadn't experienced in far too long—hope, which left him between a rock and a hard place when it came to the job he was really here to do. Did he compromise his professional integrity for this fledgling relationship or should he focus on the role he was here to complete and then walk away at the end of his time here in Royal, knowing he could be walking away from the best thing that had happened to him in a very long time?

Seven

Raina woke the next morning still locked firmly inside the bubble of joy that had enveloped her last night. Her father had taken one look at her face as she'd come into the sitting room and had shaken his head.

"I don't suppose there's any point in telling you to be careful," he'd growled from behind his beard.

She'd merely smiled and thanked her father for taking care of JJ. To his credit, he hadn't given her a lecture. Something he was inclined to do even though she was thirty years old and a mom herself. Instead he'd merely hugged her, pressed a kiss on the top of her head and, after telling her he loved her, made his way home to the trailer park.

Now Raina felt her heart skip with happiness as she made pancakes and bacon for breakfast. They needed to get some groceries this morning, her one day off, and she didn't want to waste any more time on the humdrum chore than was absolutely necessary. Today was a precious day with her boy and she wanted to make the most of it. Coaxing JJ out of his Spider-Man pajamas and into clothing suitable for the outdoors took a bit of doing but a promise to buy a new movie to add to his growing collection seemed to give him the impetus he needed.

She was in the process of buckling him into his car seat when she caught a dark movement from the corner of her eye. Raina quickly straightened up from what she was doing to see who it was who'd come up beside her. The second she did, her happy bubble burst.

Jeb.

"What are you doing here?" she demanded. "You promised you'd stay away."

"Where's my money, Raina?"

Raina quickly shoved the car door closed in an attempt to prevent JJ from hearing anything more from the man who'd done no more for him than provide a few strands of DNA.

"I don't owe you anything, Jeb Pickering. Now, please, get off my property and leave me alone."

"The boy's looking good. Growing fast. Does he ever ask about his daddy?"

"No, he doesn't," she responded flatly. God help her when JJ started asking those kinds of questions. How did you explain to your child that his father was no more than a lying no-good drifter plagued by gambling debts?

"I think it's time we met then."

"Are you threatening me?" Raina asked, her hands now clenched in tight fists of impotent rage.

Jeb had signed all the papers relinquishing his rights to any form of visitation with JJ two years ago but she should have known he'd renege on their agreement. His eyes narrowed speculatively as he looked at her car and then toward the house.

"You're doing pretty well these days, girl. I've been out

to that store of yours, too. Seems to me you could afford to help out the father of your only child, don't it?"

"You helped yourself plenty in the past. I'm done giving you money, Jeb."

Jeb's arm snaked out and his hand closed tight around Raina's wrist. She tugged against his grip, trying to free herself, but his fingers closed in a painful vice.

"Stop it. Let me go. You're hurting me," she said, pitching her voice low so there was no chance JJ could hear her. She didn't want to alarm him and from over Jeb's shoulder she could see his eyes were fixed on his mommy and the strange man talking to her.

"I need that money, honey." He gave her a crooked grin. "I'm in a bit of trouble. I need to get away. Maybe for good."

Did he mean it? She didn't dare believe him. If she showed one sign of weakness, just one, he'd exploit it. He turned back to the car and waved with his free hand toward JJ, who weakly waved back. Through the car window she could see JJ was getting upset and his muffled "Mommy?" tore at her heart.

"For good?" she pressed.

"Maybe."

"Maybe's not good enough for me, Jeb," Raina insisted, yanking her arm free. Her wrist throbbed with pain but she wouldn't look to see what damage he'd wrought. He'd done enough to her already without adding a few bruises to the list. "I don't want to ever see you again."

"Then give me my money."

His money? She stifled the urge to shove her hands hard at his chest and push him away. Give him a taste of his own medicine for a change. When had he ever had any money by honest means? She certainly couldn't remember.

"I'm mortgaged to my eyeballs with the house and I have rent to meet on my business. Pretty much everything else I have is tied up in inventory now. I don't have a lot to spare, Jeb."

"Whatever you can give me, then. And it had better be soon."

There was an urgency to his voice. An underlying thread of something he wasn't telling her, not to mention a significant threat in his tone.

"Jeb, what have you gotten yourself into now?" she sighed.

"Look, I owe a guy some cash is all. I want to clear my debts and make a fresh start."

How many times had she heard him say that? So many that she'd stopped believing him a long time ago. And look at him now. He was jittery and unkempt. Even at his worst he'd never looked this bad before. Was it really just owing money or had he gotten involved in something worse? Whatever it was, she needed to get him away from JJ as quickly as she could.

"I'll see what I can do," Raina said in defeat.

She knew it was just pandering to his dependence on her, but right now she didn't see any other way of getting rid of him. She knew she didn't have the kind of money he expected but he'd just have to make do with the couple of thousand dollars she'd put aside for emergencies when she had a chance to withdraw it from the bank. Just the thought of leaving her account empty again made her stomach burn with anxiety. All she'd ever wanted was to be able to provide her son with the same security her father had provided her—love, combined with a roof over his head, food in his belly and a warm bed at night. Was that too much to ask?

"Thanks, Rai."

"How will I be able to reach you?" The number on the mobile phone he'd been using was blocked.

"I'll be in touch."

And with that, he flipped up the collar of his jacket and began to walk away. Was it her imagination, or was he darting furtive glances left and right as he walked up the street—almost as if he expected someone to jump out of the bushes at him at any moment. She shook her head. What on earth had he got himself into, now?

She hurried to the car and, after giving JJ a shaky smile through the window, got into the driver's seat.

"Bad man, Mommy," JJ pronounced from the backseat with all the solemnity of a frightened three-year-old.

She didn't know what to say. Jeb wasn't all bad, just misguided and selfish. She settled for an indistinct murmur as she fastened her seat belt and put her key in the ignition.

"I don' like bad man. I like No'an," JJ continued.

Raina smiled at her little boy in the rearview mirror. "I like Nolan, too, honey bun. C'mon, let's go get our groceries and then the rest of the day is just for you and me."

"Yay," he crowed in happiness, his fear already forgotten.

The next morning Raina was putting out her signs at Priceless and trying to quell her excitement about the night ahead. She'd woken earlier than usual, and with an energy she could only put down to looking forward to seeing Nolan again. Even the shadow of Jeb's visit yesterday and his demands, coupled with the bruises he'd left on her wrist as a reminder, couldn't overshadow her joy in planning their dinner tonight. She'd serve lasagna with garlic bread and salad. Simple fare, and filling and, best of all, easy to prepare ahead of time so she didn't have to get herself all flustered before Nolan arrived.

As she straightened and surveyed the parking lot, she spied Mellie Winslow walking toward her. She gave the other woman a wave.

"Good morning!" she called as Mellie drew closer. "It's a lovely clear day, isn't it?"

"It is," Mellie agreed.

Her landlady looked cute today in a forest-green coat that emphasized her clear green eyes and gorgeous soft red hair. Raina envied Melanie her curls.

"Would you like to stop in for a cup of coffee?" Raina asked. "I've just put a pot on."

"I'd love that, thank you."

Mellie pulled off her gloves and shrugged out of her coat as they entered Raina's tiny lunch room. She shoved the gloves inside her coat pocket and hung the garment on one of the ornately curved brass hooks on the rack by the door.

"I love this," she said, gesturing to the rack. "And I especially love that it has an umbrella stand, as well. Is it yours or is it for sale?"

"Everything here is for sale, except me," Raina laughed in response.

"What kind of wood is it?"

"Oak. You see a lot of replicas these days, but this is the real deal."

"Hmm, maybe I should get it for Case for Christmas."

"Things are that serious?" Raina asked.

In response, Mellie thrust out her left hand, exposing a beautiful ring on her engagement finger. The large square-cut emerald gleamed under the light and Raina gasped in surprise.

"Oh, I'd say that looks very serious. Congratulations!"

"Thanks, it was all rather complicated, what with everything that went on last month, but I'm so happy."

And she looked happy, too. There was a glow about her that Raina hadn't seen before. She tried to ignore the tug of envy that plucked at her along with a wish that her own life could have followed a more traditional path. But she quickly shoved it away. Traditional or not, her life was what it was and without the choices she'd made—both good and bad—she wouldn't have JJ or be where she was now, doing something she loved.

Mellie sat down at the small table in the center of the room. "I'm glad I have a chance to talk to you today. I just wanted to let you know that I'm definitely not letting the Courtyard go. It's not for sale. Not now, not ever."

Raina felt a swell of relief flood through her. "You're serious? Everything's going to be okay?"

She'd heard, along with everyone else in town, about Homer Winslow's financial issues and how he'd put Winslow Properties into financial jeopardy. It had only served to increase her anxiety about her position here.

Mellie nodded. "Definitely. Even if Winslow Properties' resources won't stretch far enough, and I believe that with some restructuring they should, Case has assured me that he will back us financially if need be."

Raina didn't quite know what to say. She filled two coffee mugs, put them on the table with shaking hands and sank into her chair. This was incredible news.

"I'm sure you know how much this means to me, Mellie. Thank you for telling me now. It's the best Christmas present I could have imagined."

"I thought it best to give you peace of mind as soon as I knew, and I wanted to do it myself. I know how much it means to you to be here and how hard you've worked."

"But what about Samson Oil? Are they going to back off now? Seems they've been busy buying up everything that's for sale around Royal and some of what's not."

Mellie nodded her head. "Yeah, I know. It certainly looks that way, doesn't it?"

"And why? Everyone here knows the land isn't worth squat for oil, and with the drought even ranching isn't so viable. What are they thinking? Do you know who is behind it all?"

"No, all I know is that their attorney, Nolan Dane, is one stubborn guy. Every time we say no to selling, he bounces straight back with another offer. Honestly, if I hadn't taken over from Dad, Winslow Properties' portfolio would be looking very slim indeed."

Raina gasped out loud and reeled at the name that had come from Mellie's mouth. *Nolan Dane?* A giant fist clutched at her chest and squeezed tight, making it nearly impossible to draw breath.

"Raina? Are you okay?"

"I'm fine," she replied, feeling anything but. She forced herself to take a breath, drawing it all the way in before letting it out again. "A-are you sure Nolan Dane is their attorney?"

"He's certainly the person we've been dealing with. And I've heard from a few of the stall holders and retailers here that he's been sniffing around, asking all sorts of questions about the operation and about Winslow Properties. He won't have any excuse to come out here now though. Our lawyers sent him a message today categorically stating that the Courtyard is not, and never will be, for sale. At least not as long as I'm running things," Mellie confirmed before taking a long sip of her coffee. "Ah, this is good—just what I needed. I have a meeting with our board in—" she glanced at her watch "—oh, heck, twenty minutes. I'd better fly! Thanks for the coffee. I'll see myself out."

Raina remained glued to her chair in shock as Mellie put her mug in the sink, grabbed her coat and headed out of the store. Nolan was acting for Samson Oil? Did that mean that everything he'd done had been in the pursuit of getting an edge on Winslow Properties and buying the Courtyard?

She felt sick as she remembered how open she'd been about her situation. About how much all this meant to her here, to be able to start up her business again after the hellish year she'd had. And all the time he'd been planning to rip it all out from under her. Pressure built up inside her chest, growing bigger and more painful until a sob broke free. She clapped a hand over her mouth in a futile attempt to hold back the grief she felt at Nolan's betrayal.

She'd really thought he liked her—and JJ. And all along he'd simply been using them both. This hurt far worse than anything Jeb had done. He'd made empty promises, sure, but never anything like this.

Raina tipped her head back and stared at the ceiling of the old barn, willing the burning in her eyes to stop before the tears that already blinded her began to fall. Man, she could pick 'em, couldn't she? Did she have some sign over her head, visible only to losers and liars that said, "Soft touch and fool"?

After Jeb she'd sworn never again. She wouldn't make the same mistakes—not when she had JJ to consider. She'd guarded herself and her privacy, spurning male attention on the occasions it had been offered, making it clear that her son and her business were her sole priorities. Until Nolan.

He'd managed to charm his way past her barriers, slowly and gently peeling them away and exposing her vulnerability. It had been more than just the physical attraction she'd felt toward him; there'd been an emotional connection there, too. It had been so tangible that she would have sworn he felt the same way. Man, had he ever taken her for a ride.

Just went to show what an appalling judge of character she was after all. Raina dashed away an errant tear from her cheek. No. There'd be no more tears over men whose sole purpose in life was to break her heart—or worse, her hope for the future. She was better than that and she deserved better than that, too.

Raina pushed herself up onto her feet and put her mug

in the sink alongside Mellie's. She was grateful the woman had come to see her today to tell her the news. What if it had been tomorrow, or even next week? Heck, she had invited Nolan to her house for dinner with her and JJ, and who knows where that might have led given the heat of their kiss on Saturday night?

She pressed trembling fingers to her lips. It took very little stretch of her imagination to relive the pressure of his lips on hers. To remember the taste of him, the strength of his arms around her and how safe and protected he had made her feel. And that hadn't been all. He'd wanted her, she'd felt it in the hard lines of his body, and to her shame she'd wanted him back with all the heat and hunger she'd ignored for too long.

Damn him for doing this to her. For sliding under her skin and for making her want things she had no right wanting.

With a sound of disgust, Raina reached for her bag and snatched her cell phone. She pulled up Nolan's number and viciously tapped the call button on the screen. He wasn't welcome at her house anymore, let alone anywhere near her son. She had to tell him tonight was off. Tonight and every other night in the future.

Eight

Nolan pulled up outside Raina's house and sighed. Today had been tough. They'd closed on several private deals today. While on the one hand he'd known that, under the guise of Samson Oil, Rafiq was offering many people a way out of a situation that had become untenable since the tornado—people who'd been underinsured and overmortgaged and living hand-to-mouth since the disaster—he also knew he was taking them from a way of life that had been in their families for generations.

It had taken a toll—seeing relief tempered with failure, hope for a new start tempered with sorrow at leaving behind the past. These were families and people whose kids had gone to school alongside him here in Royal. And now they were scattering to the winds, some leaving Royal altogether and others settling for a life they'd never believed they'd live in one of the new suburbs. Sure, there were those who'd ecstatically accepted Rafiq's money and were eager to move forward with new lives. But the majority were people whose pride had been beaten down by so much loss that they had no fight left in them. It had been there in every hollow-eyed stare, every line of strain on their faces.

The shining light in his day today had been the knowledge that he'd see Raina again. His body had been buzzing with suppressed energy ever since Saturday night, and he'd realized that for the first time since Carole's and Bennett's deaths, he'd begun to be able to think about them without the sharp stab of pain that always accompanied the memories. Instead, he saw two new faces. Faces that he knew were fast becoming equally special to him.

Nolan got out of the SUV, hit the autolock and reached into his jacket pocket for his mobile phone before remembering he'd forgotten to charge it last night and that he'd heard the warning beeps before it shut down earlier today. It had been a blessing in disguise, he'd thought at the time, that he hadn't had to deal with the text messages and emails while he'd dotted all the *i*'s and crossed all the *t*'s on each individual contract that signaled the end of life as many people had known it. He strode up the front path—eager now to rid himself of the clinging mental residue of the day.

He'd no sooner knocked when the door was flung open. He was assailed by two things. JJ's effusive greeting, as the little boy almost knocked him off his feet with a powerful hug around his legs, and the sound of Raina's stern admonition to let her get the door. Nolan reached down and tousled JJ's mop of dark hair. An unexpected surge of tenderness swelled inside him as JJ lifted his happy little face.

"Hi, No'an."

This was what a man's life should be filled with. Moments like this that were precious and memorable for their simplicity and purity. This was what he'd been missing for far too long.

"Hey, JJ. How're you doing?"

"Good!" The little boy disengaged from Nolan's legs and began hopping from one foot to the other. "We're having lasagna for dinner. Yum!"

"JJ, let me talk to Mr. Dane," Raina interrupted, coming up behind JJ and putting a hand on his shoulder to restrain him.

Nolan's senses went on full alert. He was back to being Mr. Dane? Something was very wrong. The chill that surrounded Raina cut through JJ's excitement and the boy stilled as he looked from his mommy to Nolan in confusion.

"Do you want money from my mommy, too?" JJ asked.

Raina's eyes flared wide at her son's words, and Nolan saw the shock that streaked across her face.

"Hush, JJ. Mr. Dane doesn't want anything from me."

Oh, she was very wrong there, he thought, but he didn't miss the silent message in her words or her tone. Nolan squatted down to JJ's level and gave the little guy a reassuring smile.

"No, I don't want money from your mommy."

"You sure?"

Nolan nodded. "Of course I'm sure."

"Bad man hurt mommy."

Nolan heard Raina's gasp of shock. "JJ, don't be telling stories."

"But it true," the little boy protested.

Nolan thought it a good time to interrupt before the atmosphere got any more difficult than it was already. "Hey, JJ, look at me. I would never hurt your mommy. I promise. Okay, champ?"

JJ nodded slowly and Nolan rose to his full height again. As he did, he caught a glimpse of Raina's arm. She'd pushed the sleeves of her long-sleeved T-shirt halfway up her forearm and there was no mistaking the livid bruising around her wrist. The second she was aware he'd noticed, she pulled the sleeves down but it was too late now. He couldn't unsee what was there and he wasn't a fool. He knew fingermarks when he saw them. He'd seen marks like that, and worse, often enough when he was working alongside his father at his family law practice.

"You okay?"

Nolan chose his words carefully, even though he wished he had the right to demand who the hell had dared to lay a hand on her—and then hunt them down for some payback. Before she could answer him, though, JJ jumped up and down and started to speak.

"No'an! No'an! I'm gonna be Spider-Man at the C'istmas show!"

"Settle down, JJ," Raina admonished her son. "What he means is he's been chosen to play one of the shepherds at his day care's Christmas pageant this year."

"Yeah!" JJ interrupted again, unable to contain his excitement. "Can you come, No'an?"

"I'm sure Mr. Dane will be far too busy to attend the pageant, JJ."

Raina gave Nolan a fierce look, warning him not to contradict her. In response he squatted back down to JJ's level and put one hand on the little boy's shoulder.

"I'm sorry, JJ. Your mom is right. I'm working that night."

"I hate work!" JJ shouted, before turning tail and running down the hall toward his room.

"You mind telling me what that was about?" Nolan asked as he rose again to his full height and met Raina's chilling blue gaze full-on.

From the second he'd arrived, he'd felt a cold vibe coming from Raina that was at complete odds with the way they'd parted last time they'd been together. What the hell had gone wrong between then and now? He could have sworn that they were both heading in the same direction and now it seemed that she was slamming on the brakes. Did it have something to do with those marks on her wrist?

Again Nolan felt the slow burn of anger flicker inside at the fact that anyone had dared to lay a hand on Raina. But it was nothing compared to the irritation he felt at being manipulated into letting JJ down just now.

Raina lifted her chin and crossed her arms in front of her. Her body language was clear. She was shutting him out in more ways than one.

"Sure," she said abruptly. "I don't mind telling you. I *know* why you're here."

For a split second he was confused and then it dawned on him. She'd found out about his connection to Samson Oil. "I'm guessing it's not because of your invitation to dinner, right?"

"Don't you dare try to make a joke of it. You used me."

Nolan couldn't refute her accusation. "I'm sorry about that. Believe me, I—"

"Believe you?" she interrupted with an incredulous expression on her face. "No way. Not ever. You may have missed this in Lawyer 101, Mr. Dane, but where I come from belief comes along with trust, and I don't trust you anymore. Not now. Not after what you've been doing."

"Raina! Please? Listen to me."

"No way. Do you even understand what you were doing to me? You were working to take away my sole security. If I can't run my business at the Courtyard, JJ and I will lose everything I've worked to provide for us—we're barely making ends meet now as it is. My son deserves a bright future, one that only I can give him because God knows there's no one else there for him. By doing what you were doing, attempting to buy out that land, you threatened everything I hold dear. So, no, I won't listen to you. Not now and not ever again. Get out of my house. I don't want to ever see you here again."

Her voice broke and there were tears in her eyes as she finished her impassioned speech.

"Look, Raina, you have to let me explain—"

"The time for explanations was when you met me. Before you started pumping me for information about the Courtyard and about Royal. Not now."

The fact that she was totally right made her scorn no less galling or painful.

"Can I at least say bye to JJ?"

"No, you may not."

Raina stepped toward the front door and hauled it open. The chill air outside rushed in, enveloping them both in its icy swirl. He stared at Raina's face for a moment, but her expression remained implacable. He knew he had to pick his battles. This was definitely not the time to press her.

Silent, he passed her and went out the door. Before his feet had even struck the paved path to the road, he heard the door slam resoundingly behind him. He didn't look back, not even when he climbed into the SUV and pulled away from the curb.

On the drive back to his hotel and during a lonely dinner, he couldn't stop thinking about those bruises Raina had so swiftly hidden and who might have been responsible for them. The very idea that someone had felt they had the right to harm her like that made his blood boil and roused every protective instinct in him. Who was the bad man JJ had referred to and what was he to Raina? Was it the ex she'd said so little about? Nolan was suddenly reminded of the shadowy figure he'd seen the other night. Was it him? The thought left a sour taste in his mouth and made him determined to get to the root of what had happened to her, one way or another.

Nine

Raina was still bristling mad about Nolan's lies two days later. It had been tough breaking it to JJ that Nolan wouldn't be staying for dinner. He'd gone to bed that night grumpy and woken yesterday morning in the same state. It seemed her little guy could hold a grudge, and he laid the blame for his new idol not being around very firmly at her feet. She could only hope that the rehearsals for the pageant would distract him from his disappointment.

She thanked her lucky stars that she hadn't had time to let things go any further with Nolan than they already had. One kiss, that's all it had been—*but what a kiss*, her subconscious reminded her uncomfortably. She shoved the thought to the back of her mind and tried to focus on her preparations for the mosaic class she had scheduled tonight. Her group had enjoyed getting started on their mirror frames last week and she had no doubt that a few of them would finish gluing their pieces tonight and be ready to grout them.

She felt another flush of anger at Nolan as she remembered how his actions, if successful, would have taken all of this away from her. She hadn't been kidding when she'd told him on that first night that the Courtyard had become a symbol of hope for so many people. But then hope was obviously a cheap commodity for a man like him, along with belief and trust.

No matter how angry she was, though, she couldn't help but feel a numbing sense of loss. Her attraction to him had come out of the blue, startling her with its intensity. "Hormones, just hormones," she growled under her breath as she did her final checks around the room. Obviously she'd never learned her lesson about the kind of guy she should be attracted to. In the future, if there was any spark at all, she'd take it as a warning and then run a mile in the opposite direction. Fast.

"Hi, Raina!"

She looked up and greeted her students as they came in through the workroom's exterior door. In no time the workbenches were full. She'd had to restrict numbers on this class, as well as her Thursday night stained-glass classes purely because people needed to be able to spread their tools and supplies out while working. It was something she needed to consider when she came up with costing out her next cycle of classes in the New Year. While this first cycle had been a short one, geared mainly toward making gifts in time for Christmas, for her to maximize earnings and rebuild that little nest egg she'd had to withdraw for Jeb, she might need to have two evenings with large classes focused on smaller crafts and only one evening devoted to the larger projects.

"Okay, ladies," she said once everyone was there. "You all know where your projects are stored. I've already set out all your tools and the pots of glue and scrapers, so let's get to it!"

The noise in the workroom steadily built and conversation began to flow between the women. As Raina did her rounds, checking to make sure that everyone had what she needed and offering advice where necessary, she was startled to overhear Nolan's name being mentioned. She hated eavesdroppers but in this case she couldn't help it; she hovered near the women talking about him.

"I have to say it was a surprise to see him back in town," one of the older women said. "Apparently even his own mother didn't know he was coming back."

"Do you know why he's here? I know he's not staying with his parents. They're neighbors of mine and I've barely even seen Nolan there," replied another.

Raina interrupted them both. "He's with Samson Oil. He's the legal counsel for their land grabbing."

Her words were laced with bitterness and more than one pair of eyes swiveled to watch her as she spoke.

"Really? Oh, that's a pity. He was such a nice boy and he grew up into a fine young man."

Raina was hard pressed not to snort at the woman's remark. Fine? Sure, physically maybe. Certainly not as far as his integrity went.

The woman continued. "It was such a shame about his wife and son. A thing like that is bound to change a man. Makes him harder."

A general murmur of assent rose around her and, as if by silent mutual agreement, the women turned their conversation in a different direction. Numbing shock overwhelmed Raina, holding her paralyzed in its grip. Buzzing filled her ears. She felt herself sway a little, as if she was losing her balance, and she put out a hand to a chair to steady herself. Breathe, she told herself. Breathe. After a few seconds, she felt as if she was regaining control. Had anyone noticed how she'd completely zoned out?

She looked around the workroom. Apparently not. Her

students seemed intent on their tasks and were happily chatting among themselves while they worked. Raina drew in another breath and walked slowly to the back of the workroom where she leaned against the wall. The buzzing in her ears began to subside, but as it did, questions began circling in her mind.

A wife and son?

Nolan had never so much as mentioned his parents, let alone anyone else. Sure, he'd made vague reference to visiting family in town, but that had been it. So who was she, this wife of his? Could she have been a customer of hers, or maybe Raina had passed her in the street somewhere? And his son—how old was he?

Suddenly it all became very clear to her why Nolan was so good with her little boy. Why he hadn't been grossed out by JJ's snotty nose on the day they'd met. Why he'd so competently cleaned JJ's hands at the dinner table that night. Why he'd so easily fallen into conversation with JJ about his Spider-Man obsession.

So, were he and his wife amicably separated or bitterly estranged? Which one was it? The latter would certainly explain him staying away from Royal for so long and probably would also explain him not bringing them up in conversation. Raina clenched her hands into tight fists of frustration, digging, her fingernails into her palms. She welcomed the pain. It was a distraction from the pain of the betrayal she'd felt on learning he was working for Samson Oil—and realizing she'd let herself begin to fall for him. Hard. Physical pain she could deal with. It healed. It was the emotional pain and the toll it took that were harder to recover from.

A new thought bloomed in Raina's mind. Maybe his wife had cheated on him. Would that have been the catalyst that sent Nolan to another state? Had he sought to escape the pain of a relationship breakdown by moving away? Was that why he'd never said anything to her about a wife and child?

Whatever his circumstances, no matter whether they were justified or not, nothing excused the way he'd sought her out under false pretenses. He'd deceived her about the Courtyard. Why wouldn't he do the same about a wife and child, too? It wasn't her problem. Not anymore. She'd sent him on his way and it was highly unlikely their paths would cross again.

Nolan was glad of the excuse to quit Royal, even if it was for only one day to meet with his boss in Holloway. He'd known coming back to Royal would be tough, would force him to face a lot of his personal demons, but he hadn't expected, or wanted, to find someone to whom he was so strongly attracted.

He struck the steering wheel with the heel of his palm and cursed aloud in the cabin of the SUV. How could he have handled things differently with Raina? No matter how many times he examined everything they'd said and done since he'd met her, he still couldn't see anywhere he could have prevented what happened. Short of telling her exactly why he was in Royal on the day he'd introduced himself at the Courtyard, of course. And he'd just bet how well that would have gone down.

Besides, the confidentiality clause in his contract with Rafiq prevented him from disclosing Samson Oil's business with anyone other than the party with whom he was negotiating. His hands had been tied.

Even though he'd rationalized everything, he still couldn't erase the look on Raina's face when she'd told him to get out of her house. He'd dealt with a lot of angry people in his time, but never before had there been such a palpable level of anguish beneath the anger. It had tortured him to know he'd put that look on her face.

He knew he should have stepped away the moment he'd recognized the fierce attraction he'd felt toward her. How often had he told himself that she was everything he *wasn't* looking for?

A speed limit sign shot by his window and Nolan realized that he'd been so lost in his thoughts that he'd lost track of what he was doing. He eased off the accelerator and focused on his surroundings. He was almost there. As much as he wasn't looking forward to imparting the news to Rafe that the Courtyard was completely off the table, it would at least be some respite from constantly thinking about Raina.

The entrance to the Holloway Inn wasn't what Nolan had expected. From the moment he pulled up outside, he wondered if somewhere along the line he hadn't somehow traveled thousands of miles to England. The white stucco walls, with dark wooden battens, reminded him very much of a Tudor inn he and Carole had stayed in outside London during their honeymoon, although, he noted as he entered the lobby, that's where the similarities ended. There'd be no ducking to clear doorways here. He walked up to the reception desk and smiled at the receptionist.

"Good morning. Nolan Dane to see Mr. Ben Samson," he said, using the name Rafe had assumed while the property negotiations were ongoing.

"Welcome to the Holloway Inn, Mr. Dane. Mr. Samson is waiting for you in his suite."

The young woman smiled and gave him concise directions to the suite, and Nolan located the rooms without any trouble. His knock was quickly answered by Rafe himself. The fact his boss was alone was unusual but not entirely unexpected given how secretive he'd been about his involvement with Samson Oil from the outset.

"Good morning," Rafe said, shaking Nolan's hand and gesturing for him to enter. "Knowing how punctual you always are, I took the liberty of ordering coffee already. Help yourself."

"Thank you."

Nolan stepped inside, his feet sinking into the plush carpeting. He looked around the suite. It was no more and no less than he'd come to expect. The main living room was spacious and well lit. A fifty-inch flat-screen television took pride of place on one wall and a number of oversize leather sofas and chairs were grouped around it. Across the room, a dining table, large enough to comfortably seat twelve, was covered in what looked like a map of Royal and several stacks of papers.

He gave Rafe a look. His boss was as immaculately turned out as ever but there were shadows under his eyes.

"Hard night?" he asked, as he poured himself a coffee and helped himself to a Danish pastry from the white-linen-draped room-service cart.

"I met someone."

Rafe's terse response was characteristic of the man himself, but the second he reached for the cuff of his sleeve and gave it a tug, Nolan knew there was a great deal of meaning behind those three words. Rafe was a controlled man and generally very reserved. In fact, the first time Nolan had met him he'd been a little unnerved by the guy's intensity until he learned to appreciate the keen intelligence and mind for business that lay behind it. But he had his familiar mannerisms, as well, and Nolan knew this one—something had made Rafiq uncomfortable. Something… or someone.

"A woman?" Nolan pressed before taking a sip of his coffee.

"Of course a woman," Rafe laughed. "An intriguing and beautiful one at that."

"Have I met her before?"

"I only met her myself last night."

For a second Rafe's eyes got a faraway look, as if he was remembering something intensely personal.

In all the time Nolan had worked for his boss, he'd never known the man to indulge in anything as impulsive as a one-night stand. He wouldn't mind meeting the woman who'd managed to put that look in his boss's eye.

"She must have been something else, huh?" he probed.

"Yes, she certainly was." Rafe appeared to shake off whatever memory had gripped him and gathered himself together. "But that's in the past. We're not here to discuss my after-hours activities. Come, sit at the table. Bring me up to date. What's happening with Winslow Properties?"

Shaking his head, Nolan settled into a chair while Rafiq took one opposite. "No movement there at all. We don't stand a chance under the new management. It's like arguing with a wooden Indian."

Rafe raised one dark brow and Nolan waved a hand in response.

"Local terminology," he explained. "Basically, pressing forward with Winslow Properties is a waste of time. They're not selling."

Rafe didn't look pleased. "You're certain?"

"Absolutely."

To his credit Rafe accepted the news with better grace than Nolan had anticipated. Perhaps he realized that sometimes it was better to step away. Rafe pushed a folder toward Nolan.

"Let's move on these, then."

Nolan lifted the folder from the table and opened it. He ran his eye down the list on the first sheet. Not entirely surprising, he thought, and from what he'd seen and heard in Royal already, he had no doubt they'd manage to acquire these properties without too much hassle. His eye stopped on the name of one ranch, though, and a frisson of disquiet tickled at the back of his mind.

"All of these?" Nolan asked, looking up from the documents.

Not a man to waste words, Rafe merely nodded.

"This one—the Wild Aces ranch—what do you want with that?"

Again Rafe raised one brow. "I don't pay you to ask questions."

Nolan's sense of unease increased. He'd done plenty of research both before he returned to Royal and since he'd been there. He knew who was vulnerable and he knew who'd had enough hardship to be coaxed off their land and sent to newer pastures. And he knew, without a doubt, that with the right amount of coercion, the owners of the Wild Aces would in all likelihood accept a reasonable offer for their land.

"That's true," Nolan conceded. "But if I'm to perform my role properly, I need to know the background."

Rafe met Nolan's gaze full-on, not giving an inch and continuing to say nothing. Eventually Rafe made a sound of annoyance and leaned forward, placing his elbows on the table between them and steepling his fingers.

"Why is it so important to you all of a sudden to know why? It hasn't been an issue for you up until now."

"I'm your boots-on-the-ground man. As such, I'm a lot closer to the people of Royal."

"Which is exactly why I appointed you to this role. You grew up there. You know how best to attain my goals."

"But I don't know why you're doing this. People are already asking questions. Questions I can't answer."

"And you don't have to."

"No, that's true. But my parents still live there. My father still practices there. I would hate there to be any fallout for them."

"There will be no fallout. Are we not helping people by relieving them of useless assets? Offering them good money and a fresh start before they're forced to move on when their banks foreclose?"

"We are. But if the assets are so useless, why do you want them so badly?"

Rafe said nothing.

"If I'm to continue to act on your behalf I need to know."

Rafe leaned back in his chair again. "A threat, Nolan?"

"No, a statement of fact. Take Wild Aces for example. Most of that land is leased out to another operation, the McCallums', because their stored water supply was compromised after the tornado and with the drought they haven't been able to replenish their water stock. To keep their herds at optimum levels, they're leasing this land here." He stabbed a finger at the map on the table. "If your offer to purchase the land is accepted by the owners, do you intend to continue with the lease already in place?"

"My plans are mine alone. I don't disclose my reasons." Rafe paused before adding, "To anyone."

Nolan carefully closed the folder in his hands and, equally carefully, placed it on the table. "Then I cannot continue to work for you."

"You're serious?"

"Never more so. I will not represent Samson Oil unless I have a better understanding of what your aims are in relation to the land acquisitions. Like I said, people are beginning to ask questions and I have a few of my own."

"It is no one's business but mine."

There were times when Rafe's privileged background shone through—times like this when he held himself above others and believed his will was law. That might be the case back in Al Qunfudhah, his homeland, but the last time Nolan checked it certainly wasn't that way in Texas.

"Then I'm sorry, but I'm forced to resign. Effective immediately."

"We have a contract, Nolan," Rafe reminded him. "You are bound to honor that, are you not?"

"A contract I drew up," Nolan said on a sigh. "And under the terms of the exit clause, I believe you'll discover that I'm within my rights to do this. I'm sorry, Rafe. I've always liked you and admired your business acumen, but I can no longer continue to work for you. Not under these circumstances. I hope we can still be friends."

He rose and extended his hand. Rafe hesitated a moment before also getting to his feet and clasping Nolan's hand in return.

"I, too, am sorry it has come to this. Can I ask you one thing?"

"What's that?"

"Why? You were happy to continue working under my instructions before. What changed?"

Nolan gave Rafe a bitter smile. "I met someone."

Ten

Nolan drove away from Holloway with a sense of lightness he hadn't felt in a very long time. It was as if walking away from his contract with Rafiq had freed him from an invisible cell. It wasn't that he hadn't enjoyed his work, because he had. He'd always loved the cut and thrust of law, and property law had brought its own challenges to keep him sharp. But he'd never truly stopped to consider the peripheral effect of what he was doing. Not until he'd met Raina.

Would she allow him back into her life? He wanted to tell her he was no longer acting for Samson Oil, but after the way they'd parted, he seriously doubted that he could just pull up to her front door and expect her to see him.

He activated the hands-free calling in his car and spoke her name. Through the speaker he heard the phone at the other end begin to ring.

Pick up, he silently willed her. *Pick up.* But after a few short rings, the call was diverted to voice mail. He was disappointed but not surprised. In fact, he wouldn't have put it past her to have blocked his number altogether.

Nolan left a message anyway, asking her to please call him when she had a chance. As he ended the call he wondered whether she would call him back. Maybe she'd simply delete his message without listening to it. Well, he'd call her back again. Not too soon, of course. Even he respected that he'd done a serious amount of damage when it came to her trust in him. He had a lot of work to do before he won it back.

At a bit of a loose end, Nolan decided to drop in on his parents. Maybe his dad needed some wood chopped. He sure hoped so, because he suddenly had a burning urge to work off some energy and wood chopping felt like just the chore for it.

When he got to his parents' house, he sat in the car a moment and stared at the home where he'd grown up. He had so many memories from when he was a kid and more from when he'd reached his teens. He still remembered, clear as day, the first time he'd brought Carole over to meet his mom and dad. He and Carole had been in their last year of high school, each with the same goal for their future. Even then they'd hoped to build that future together.

Would he have changed anything if he could? He'd known Carole for what felt like forever, but he still remembered the day when he'd seen her and everything had changed. It was as if a switch had been thrown in his mind and from that moment forward he'd known she was the one for him. It turned out that he'd been a little slow on the uptake. She'd decided long before that she wanted him, too, and she'd waited patiently, biding her time until he woke up to the fact that they'd been made for one another.

Strange how he could think about her now without it hurting. Yes, he still missed her and he probably always would, but he could also remember the good times—the fun times before life got so frenetic and busy and pressured and everything fell apart. Before their son had died and she'd taken her own life in a cruel combination of guilt and grief and hopelessness.

A movement on the front porch of his parents' house dragged Nolan from his reveries. His dad—standing there in the cold, quite happy to wait until his son was ready to get out of the car in which he'd been sitting for, he now realized, upward of twenty minutes while his thoughts wandered.

Nolan finally got out of the SUV and walked up the front path. His dad greeted him with a hug. Although Nolan was a grown man, he still took succor from his father's grasp, from the warmth and unconditional love.

"Everything okay, son?" Howard Dane asked him.

Nolan met his father's brown eyes, so like his own, and smiled. "Yeah, Dad. Everything's okay."

His father gave him a nod. "Your mother was worried when she saw you parked out front. You know what she's like."

"I was thinking. About Carole and Bennett."

His father's eyes dulled with unspoken pain. "Thought as much. It's why we left you to it."

"So," Nolan said, clapping his father on the back as they turned and walked toward the front door. "Got any wood that needs chopping?"

His father laughed. "In that suit? I don't think so."

"Maybe you can loan me something to wear."

Howard Dane eyed him up and down. "Maybe I can. You look like a stuffed shirt, son."

"Not anymore, Dad. Not anymore."

Nolan's back and shoulders ached like he couldn't remember and the blisters on the palms of his hands reminded him he'd grown soft during his time in California.

It had been good to do some manual labor. It gave him plenty of time for thinking. His mom had brought out some lunch for him and his dad, who was busy stacking the firewood as Nolan split the logs. Once they were done and came inside, Nolan looked across the sitting room and saw the new gas fireplace installed where the old open fire had once been. He turned and looked at his father.

"You didn't tell me you'd gotten rid of the old fireplace."

His father shrugged. "Sometimes a man just has to chop wood."

Nolan gave his father a look. "Why'd you have it removed?"

"Debris from the tornado damaged the old chimney. We decided to remove the whole thing, fireplace and all."

"You might have told me." Nolan laughed.

His dad shrugged again. "It's no bother. Besides, the wood should come in handy come summer. Your mother made me buy one of those fancy brazier things for the back patio. We'll use it for that."

Nolan laughed again. This was what he'd missed living so far away. His father's quiet acceptance and solid support. It didn't mean he was a pushover. No sirree. In fact, Howard Dane was known through several counties as a tough lawyer who could be relied on to stand up for his clients.

Nolan's mother came through from the kitchen.

"Are you staying for dinner?" she asked, wiping her hands dry on a tea towel.

"I'd like that if you have room for me," he said with a wink that he knew would earn an eye roll in response. He wasn't disappointed.

"Go get cleaned up and I'll see if we can squeeze you in at the table," his mother teased, flicking the tea towel in his direction.

Over dinner, Nolan told his parents about his decision to quit Samson Oil.

"So what are you going to do now?" his mom asked with a worried frown on her still-pretty face.

"I haven't given it a lot of thought yet, Mom. I just made the decision today."

"But it's not like you not to have a plan beforehand. What on earth prompted you to do such a thing?"

Nolan eyed both his parents before answering. "I didn't feel comfortable with it anymore. Yes, I know we were doing a lot of good, giving people a way out they didn't have before. But somewhere along the line, others would get hurt and I figure Royal's seen enough hurt already. I just couldn't do it anymore."

His father narrowed his eyes at him and Nolan shifted in his seat. Howard was a man of few words but when he chose them, you generally listened.

"What changed?"

Not, why did *you* change, Nolan observed of his father's question. It made him think carefully about his response.

"I guess it mattered to me more."

His father continued to look at him in much the same way he had back when Nolan was a kid and had done something wrong. Howard knew that silence was a very effective weapon.

"I met someone. Someone who reminded me of what it's like to feel." Nolan heard his mother's gasp of surprise, but he kept going. "Someone who potentially was going to be put at a major disadvantage both financially and emotionally if things had continued the way they were. Regrettably, I withheld information from her. I abused her trust. I don't like the man who did that and I don't want to be that person anymore."

"Good to hear, son. So who do you want to be now?" Howard said quietly.

"The man who makes things right again."

Nolan watched his father take a sip of his wine and set the glass carefully back down on his mother's crisp white linen tablecloth.

His father sighed and looked up at him again. "And if you can't?"

Nolan shook his head. Failure wasn't an option. He wouldn't be his father's son if it was. "I will succeed. It won't be easy, but I'll get there."

"Does she know about your old life here?"

"No, and I need to address that. She deserves to hear it from me. It's just…not easy talking about them."

"You'll find the right time, son, and the right words," his father said encouragingly.

"Does this mean you're moving back to Royal for good?" his mom asked while she gathered up the plates from the table.

"I hope so," Nolan answered. "No, I know so. LA isn't the right place for me. Not anymore. It was a good place to run to. It let me grieve at my own pace and in private. But I'm back now."

Howard shifted in his seat. "You planning to set up a property law practice here?"

Nolan shook his head. "No. In fact, I think I'm ready to go back to my roots, to family law." He gave his father a half smile. "Do you know anyone looking for a lawyer?"

His father's smile was slow to come but when it did, it shone with a world of approval and joy. "I think I might know of a space. You'd have to brush up a bit, jump through a few hoops, untie some red tape."

"Oh, Howard, stop teasing the boy," Nolan's mom protested. "You know you need him back at the practice. It hasn't been the same since he left."

Nolan met his dad's gaze and stood as Howard rose to his feet. The older man extended his hand across the table and Nolan grasped it firmly, exactly the way his father had taught him more years ago than he could even remember.

"Then, welcome back aboard, son. We've missed you."

"It's good to be back, Dad. Thank you."

And Nolan knew the words were more than just that. Inside he felt as if everything had clicked back into place. Almost everything, he corrected himself. There was still some rebuilding to do, if that was even possible. But, like he'd reminded himself before, failure wasn't an option.

Number withheld. Raina stared at her cell phone screen and debated taking the call. It was quiet in the store; she had no reason not to take it, and yet there was a knot in her stomach that made her hesitate. She knew it wasn't Nolan. He'd been leaving messages every day since Saturday asking her to call him. She wished she had the courage to call him back and tell him to stop calling her, or even had the courage to block his number, but something always held her back. That same perverse something that gave her a quiet thrill of attraction every time she heard his voice.

Her phone went silent in her hand and a few seconds later the icon popped up telling her she had a voice message. With a sigh of frustration, Raina checked it. And there it was, she thought as she listened. Yet another call from Jeb. She'd already told him how much money she could give him but he insisted on more. Telling her his life depended on it. When she'd pressed him for details, he'd explained about the gambling debts he'd incurred in New Mexico. The loans he'd taken out with some guy who was now impatient to be repaid. The sum had staggered her. Surely Jeb couldn't have gambled it all away?

She had the impression that for all the things he'd told her, he was still holding something back. She decided it was time to get to the root of it and dialed the number he'd given her in his message.

"Rai, about time," he growled in her ear.

"What aren't you telling me?" Raina demanded, not wasting any time on pleasantries.

"Babe, I've told you everything you need to know."

Need to know? She looked to the ceiling of the old barn and prayed for strength. "Look, I might be able to borrow some money from my dad. But you have to tell me the truth, Jeb. Why so much?"

He laughed, a grating sound that was devoid of even an ounce of mirth. "I've gotta get out, Rai. Disappear and never come back. That costs."

Disappear? Never come back? Heck, if she believed—even for one minute—that he'd never be back it would be worth paying him what he was asking. To think that she wouldn't have to be wondering and waiting when the next call or visit would come. The next demand for more money. But what on earth had he done that was so bad?

"Forever?" she asked, the word slipping from her mouth before she even realized she'd said it.

"Aw, Rai, don't tell me you're gonna miss me. Or is it maybe that you really don't want to see me ever again?"

Raina shuddered. He was back to playing his word games, twisting everything around, including her, until she didn't know which way was up anymore.

"How much? Tell me, Jeb. Exactly how much do you need?"

He named a sum that had her rocking back on her heels. "I can't do that."

"That's what it's gonna take, Rai baby. And I need it by tomorrow."

"Tomorrow?" She couldn't get that kind of cash together by tomorrow and she doubted that even if her dad was prepared to lend her the money he could either. Besides, tomorrow was JJ's pageant. She didn't want Jeb anywhere near her or her son on what was a very important day for her little boy. "That's far too soon! Give me a few days."

"I don't have a few days." Jeb's tone became more urgent and a shiver of fear trickled down Raina's spine. "I'll see you tomorrow. Look out for me."

With that he hung up, leaving Raina staring at her phone and shaking. How on earth had she ever let things get to this? She should have drawn the line on being his cash cow years ago, but somehow it had always been easier just to pay him and send him on his way.

Raina stared at her phone and knew she had to do this. She dialed her father's number. He answered on the second ring.

"Dad, I need your help."

Eleven

Raina had been on tenterhooks all day. Her father, bless him, had come to see her at the store earlier in the day with a wad of bills. That he'd done such a thing, even knowing that the money was for Jeb, filled her heart with gratitude. No matter what happened in her life, she had him as her rock. When her mother had abandoned her, he'd been there. When Jeb had abandoned her, he'd been there. Every minute of every day that she needed him. But he wasn't getting any younger and it was time she was that rock for him, not the other way around. She needed to be able to stand on her own two feet.

And then there was the anxiety of carrying several thousand dollars in cash on her person for the rest of the day. Every time someone had come into the store and set the bell above the door ringing, she'd virtually jumped out of her skin. By the time she'd closed up shop and headed home, her nerves had been stretched so taut she felt as if the slightest thing would see her fracture into a million pieces.

"Mommy! Mommy! Look, I'm Spider-Man!" JJ zoomed around the house in his costume, looking like no shepherd any children's pageant had ever seen.

"JJ, we've talked about this. You can't be Spider-Man in the pageant," she said wearily and with an edge to her voice that JJ didn't miss.

"I am, Mommy. I am!"

His face took on a petulant look that reminded her all too much of his father, and Raina was hard pressed to remind herself not to visit her frustrations over Jeb's sins upon JJ. She had to pick her battles.

"How about you be Spider-Man in the car and then a shepherd when we get to the hall?"

"Spider-Man!" JJ shouted and hopped on one foot.

"C'mon," Raina said, fighting to hold on to her temper. "Let's get your coat on. If we don't go soon we'll be late."

By the time she had them both bundled up and in the car her hands were shaking. She took in several steadying breaths before putting the car in Reverse and backing out of the drive, all the time keeping an eye out for Jeb. But he was nowhere to be seen. She didn't know whether to be relieved or sorry.

Luck was finally with her when they got to the hall where the pageant was being staged and she parked her car in the last vacant space in the lot. Uttering a silent prayer of thanks, Raina helped JJ from the car and grabbed his shepherd's costume before heading toward the foyer. Inside was a cluster of angels on one side, shepherds on the other and all other variety of pageant costumes in between. And Spider-Man, Raina told herself. Don't forget him.

A tingle of awareness spread through her body as she sensed a movement to her right-hand side. Jeb?

"No'an!" JJ cried.

Raina felt her body sag. Was it in relief or in shock that he'd come? Right now he was definitely the lesser of two evils.

"Raina, I hope you don't mind me being here, but I didn't want to let JJ down."

"The pageant is open to everyone," she replied. "Just a small donation is requested for the local food bank."

"I know, I've already donated," Nolan said.

Just then, someone jostled her from behind, making her lose her balance, and Nolan immediately steadied her, his large warm hands at her shoulders. He let go of her just as soon as she was steady on her feet and for some stupid reason, tears sprang to her eyes. Raina blinked furiously to rid herself of them. She'd weathered tough days before and this one wasn't any different, she reminded herself.

A call went out for the shepherds to assemble and to go with one of the day care teachers.

"C'mon, JJ," Raina said, shaking out his costume. "Let's get you changed."

"No. I'm Spider-Man, Mommy."

JJ's voice was raised and Raina saw several faces turn toward them. Her cheeks flushed with embarrassment.

"Maybe we should just go home," she muttered to herself but JJ overhead her and pitched his voice so that everyone in the foyer could hear him.

"No! Not going home!"

JJ was normally an even-tempered child but when he threw a tantrum it had force equal to the tornado that had leveled so much of Royal more than a year ago. On top of everything she'd dealt with in the situation with Jeb, this was one thing too many for Raina. She reached for JJ's hand, determined to take him back out to the car, drag him if she had to, but Nolan put a hand on her arm.

"Maybe I can help," he offered, taking the shepherd

costume from her and squatting down in front of JJ. "Hey, champ, you've blown your cover."

JJ eyed Nolan with a wary but intrigued expression.

Nolan gave JJ a serious look. "No one knows who Spider-Man really is, right? He hides his suit until his special powers are needed, doesn't he?"

JJ nodded slowly, his eyes growing wide.

"Quick," Nolan suggested. "Before anyone notices. Let's cover you up."

To Raina's stunned surprise, JJ let Nolan dress him in the rough cotton overshirt, complete with rope belt, and secured the tea towel she'd brought for his head with another length of twine.

"Great work," Nolan whispered to the little boy. "I think your secret is safe."

"Raina, is JJ ready?" one of the day care teachers asked, clipboard in hand and a harried expression on her face. "Oh, great, I see he is. That's everyone accounted for. I'll bring him out back so you can go and take your seat."

Before she knew it, JJ was amiably holding hands with his teacher and walking away. But all of a sudden he broke free and ran back to Nolan and beckoned for him to lean down. Her little boy whispered something in Nolan's ear and gave him a massive hug around his neck.

This time Raina couldn't hold back the tear that spilled over and traced a line down her cheek. She brushed it away but not before Nolan noticed it.

"Thank you," she said to him, her voice shaking just a little.

Nolan didn't say anything right away, just pushed his hands in his trouser pockets and looked at her. Raina self-consciously looked away. She wasn't at her best tonight. A sleepless night followed by the tension of today, capped off by JJ's behavior, had left her feeling more raw and vulnerable than she had in a long time.

"Raina, we need to talk."

"No." She shook her head. "No we don't. Thank you for settling JJ for me, but we've said all we need to say to one another. And, to be honest, the time for you to *talk* to me was when we met. Not now."

She turned to go but Nolan caught the sleeve of her coat.

"Please, Raina. Just give me five minutes. You won't answer or return my calls—what else was I supposed to do but turn up to see you?"

"So you didn't come here for JJ then?" She challenged him with an angry glare.

"Of course I came for JJ. But I'd have been stupid not to want to see you, too."

Raina crossed her arms over her chest. "Fine. Say what you've come to say."

Nolan looked around the busy foyer full of parents and family members of the performers all milling about. "Can we step outside for a bit of privacy?"

He held his breath, waiting for Raina's reply, and felt a surge of relief when she gave him a brief nod and headed toward the main doors. They found a spot outside under the portico where they wouldn't be in the way of people coming into the hall. She still had her arms crossed and her eyes kept flicking this way and that, as if she was on the lookout for someone.

"Thank you," he said. "I appreciate it."

"Just get to the point, Nolan. What is it that you're so determined to tell me?"

While she still sounded as if she was madder at him than a wet hen, he could see she was barely holding herself together. Lines of strain pulled around her mouth and eyes and she looked exhausted.

"I've quit Samson Oil," he started, thinking he may as well get to the point from the beginning. She definitely wasn't in a mood to mess around. "I thought a lot about what you said and you were right. It made me look at myself with fresh eyes and I didn't like what I saw anymore."

Raina didn't respond, so he continued.

"I've decided to move back to Royal, to rejoin my father's practice. I know I can do good there and while I feel that I did a lot of good with Samson Oil, I also hurt a lot of people, too. Especially you. I'm sorry for that, Raina. It was never my intention to cause you any harm either directly or indirectly. Nor could I just stand aside and let my boss potentially harm people like you anymore."

Raina shifted from one foot to the other and rubbed her upper arms with her hands. It was clear she'd heard about all she was prepared to listen to.

"Why is this any of my business, Nolan? What makes you think I care where you live or what you do?"

The hurt was there, loud and clear in every word she spoke even though she'd kept her tone even.

"I'd like to think it's your business because before I messed everything up, you started to have feelings for me." At her sound of protest he continued. "The way I have feelings for you. Hear me out, please. Raina, I think I'm falling in love with you. Yes, I know it's sudden and that we barely know one another but from the first moment I laid eyes on you I knew you were someone special. Someone who had been missing in my life. Please, give me another chance. Give *us* another chance."

He waited for her response for what felt like forever, even though he logically knew it could only have been a minute or so. Her face had changed, become unreadable even to someone like him who was used to studying every nuance of expression for answers. Finally, she took in a breath and spoke.

"I can't make a decision about something like that here and now."

He took solace in the fact that it wasn't a direct no.

"I accept that. Look, right now it's enough that you're prepared to think about it."

"I need to get inside. They'll be starting soon."

She pushed past him and he let her go. It would probably be too much to expect her to sit with him. Nolan watched her go in the front doors and started, more slowly, to follow. He didn't care if he stood at the back of the hall for the duration of the pageant, but he would be there for JJ. As he made his way to the door, he saw a shadow detach itself from the bushes near the road. Nolan watched as the man walked toward the parking area. There was something about the shape and size of the man, and the way he moved, that was vaguely familiar. In a rush, Nolan remembered the person he'd seen on the road near Raina's house.

Every sense in his body went on full alert. He followed the man to the lot where he saw the guy draw to a halt by Raina's car.

"Can I help you?" he called out and was surprised when the guy wheeled around to face him rather than run away.

The man's face might once have been handsome, Nolan thought, but the dissipation wrought by hard living, no doubt compounded by too much alcohol judging by the smell coming from him right now, had left its mark.

"I know you," the man said. "Seen you sniffing around Raina's place. She's a fine piece of ass, isn't she?"

Nolan's hands curled into fists at the familiar way the man spoke about Raina.

"What's it to you?" he demanded.

The guy laughed. "She hasn't told you about me, has she? Her dirty little secret."

Suddenly it all started to slip into place. This guy was Raina's ex—and JJ's father. Nolan instinctively wanted to shield them from this guy—to make sure he didn't touch or tarnish their lives again. But, last he checked, murder was still illegal in the state of Texas.

"I know about you," Nolan said, taking scant satisfaction in pricking Jeb Pickering's bubble of confidence. This was the man who'd left Raina's wrist looking black and blue. Nolan itched to deliver a dose of the same thing to the bastard but he knew there were ways and means of dealing with lowlifes like him—and he was going to make sure he never hurt Raina again. "You're not wanted here. Get on your way."

"I got every right to be here. More right 'n you, anyways. JJ's my boy. Not yours."

Jeb's stance altered and he drew himself up to his full height in an effort to intimidate Nolan. While the guy had an inch or two on him, Nolan knew that if it came to it, he'd still best Pickering in a fight. That, however, would be a last resort.

"Now you want to claim him?" Nolan sneered. "A bit late, isn't it?"

"It's never too late," Jeb challenged in return.

"It is when you're a no-good waste of time. You think you're a man but you're nothing. A real man doesn't treat a woman the way you've treated Raina."

Jeb's expression grew ugly under the lamp light, his mouth twisting into a harsh line. "You don't know nothing 'bout what happened."

"I know enough."

The look on Jeb's face changed again, going from belligerent to sly in one breath.

"A man can change his mind, can't he? Although—" he paused and rubbed at the stubble on his chin "—I guess that would mess up your plans, wouldn't it?"

"My plans?"

Nolan inwardly cursed himself for falling into Jeb's verbal trap.

"Yeah, your plans with my girl and my son."

"Look, you might be his biological father but be honest, that's where your attachment to JJ begins and ends. As for Raina, she's not your girl. Not anymore."

"Ah, but she's not yours either, is she? Not yet."

Jeb looked smug and Nolan's hands itched to wipe that expression off his face.

"Besides," Jeb continued. "She owes me."

Nolan shook his head. "I don't see how she owes you anything."

"Money, doofus. She owes me money. We have, what you would say, an agreement."

"Haven't you already taken enough from her? What kind of man are you anyway, constantly leeching off a woman that way?"

The insult fell on deaf ears. "I'm here to get what's mine. Mind you, since you're the one who has the hots for Rai, maybe *you* should be the one paying me."

He could imagine the gears grinding in the back of Jeb's mind as the man took in Nolan's appearance, the quality of his coat, the expensive haircut and his handmade boots. Since money was the man's major motivator, Nolan hoped that maybe he could save Raina the additional pressure of ever having to see Jeb again. Maybe.

"How much?" Nolan demanded.

"Look, man, this is between Raina and me," Jeb started, rocking back on his feet slightly. "But if you wanted to pay what she owes me—hell, I'm an equal opportunity kind of guy. Your money is as good as hers."

"If I give you anything, you have to give me your word, such as it is, that you won't bother Raina again."

"Hey, man, no need to insult me," Jeb protested, suddenly the picture of a man affronted when his integrity has been called into question. But then he laughed. It was an ugly sound that revealed his true avaricious character. "Whatever. When can you pay me?"

"First you have to tell me how much."

Jeb named a figure and Nolan didn't so much as bat an eyelid. "I can do that. Give me your bank account details."

"I don't have no bank account, man. I need cash and I need it now."

"I can get it to you tomorrow night. But on one condition."

"What's that?"

"That you get away from here now and stay away from Raina and JJ."

"It's not like I want to see them," Jeb scowled. "She owes me, is all. But, yeah, I'll do as you say. She won't see me—tonight anyway."

"Good. But if I hear that she's caught so much as a glimpse of you after our talk tonight, the deal's off." Nolan glared at him to make his point clear. "And I'll make sure she doesn't give you anything either."

Jeb looked at him, as if trying to figure out whether Nolan could influence Raina that much. Obviously he decided that Nolan could. He lifted his chin in acceptance of the terms.

"Where d'you want to meet?"

Nolan named a parking lot in back of some buildings downtown. Jeb nodded. "I know it. I'll be there. Six o'clock tomorrow night. Don't be late or the deal's off and I'm back to my original plan."

"Oh, I'll be on time, don't you worry about that," Nolan affirmed, staying outside to watch Jeb as he headed off down the street and faded from sight.

Nolan went back to the hall. The lights gleaming on the front porch were a welcome contrast to the darkness of the man he'd just seen leave. He wondered what the hell Raina had ever seen in Jeb Pickering, but then again, knowing her even as little as he did, he could see why the lost boy inside Jeb would appeal to her nature to nurture and mend what was broken. She certainly had mended what was broken within him, Nolan thought, and made him dream of a new future.

He quietly let himself into the hall and scanned the rows of seats, trying to spot Raina. There she was. Again that familiar wave of protectiveness swept through him. Dealing with Jeb would be an unpleasant business, but he'd do whatever it took to keep Raina safe from that creep and anything or anyone else that threatened her. Raina and JJ both.

As if she'd sensed his presence, she turned and their eyes met. She gave him a tentative smile and waved him to come toward her. Nolan realized she'd saved him a seat. The knowledge eased loose the knot he'd been carrying in his chest since she'd confronted him and told him to get lost, and for the first time in a long time, Nolan admitted he felt hope.

Twelve

From the moment Nolan sat down next to her, Raina felt every nerve and cell in her body become attuned to his nearness. The seats were close together so his broad shoulder brushed against hers. In the end, it was easier to give in to the occasional contact and stop trying to hold herself apart from him.

Who was she kidding anyway? Yes, she was still mad at him and, yes, she still felt betrayed, but he'd extended an olive branch tonight. While her first instinct had been to reject it, and him, in an attempt to save herself from any further hurt or heartbreak, didn't she owe it to herself to give him another chance? If what he said was true, and he'd quit Samson Oil, maybe that was the genuine measure of the man himself.

She glanced toward him and caught him looking back at her. His brown eyes were alight with joy and she felt her body relax even more.

"Our Spider-Man is doing great, don't you think?" he whispered to her, leaning in closer.

Her nostrils flared as his scent wafted toward her, making her insides twist with suppressed need. It was all she could do to smile and nod an acknowledgment and return her eyes to the stage where JJ stood as tall and proud as he could, his little face turned to the crowd and his gaze searching for her among the many faces. She saw the moment he picked her out in the crowd and he beamed at her, and then his eyes drifted to where Nolan sat beside her and she thought JJ's face might split with happiness.

She felt a telltale prickle of tears in her eyes. She'd tried so darn hard to be everything that JJ had needed in his young life. But his obvious joy at having Nolan present made her realize that she couldn't be all things to her son, no matter what she did. Not being able to ensure he had the best of everything life had to offer frustrated her. She wanted him to have it all.

If Nolan's words were true, if he was really falling in love with her, then she had to know how he felt about JJ, too. They were a package deal.

But what of the wife and child she'd heard mention of earlier this week? How could she casually bring that up in conversation without it sounding as if she'd been snooping into his life? Of course, she rationalized, she had a right to snoop—she had more than herself to consider—but snooping had never been her thing. She'd always been a "live and let live" type of person, someone who tried to always see the good in people.

But hadn't that very facet of her personality caused her to make some of the worst decisions in her life, as well? Decisions like Jeb and the loser boyfriends she'd had before him? No—no matter which way she looked at it, she couldn't regret her time with Jeb no matter how much it had cost her and how much heartache he'd wrought. Without him, she wouldn't have had JJ. Becoming a parent had made her realize just what her father had sacrificed for her all these years and deepened her love for him a thousandfold. Her dad had worked hard to make up for her mother's abandonment, and while he'd had lady friends come and go through the years, Raina had never felt as if she'd lacked for not having her mother with her growing up.

Which brought her to even more questions. Was it in JJ's best interests for her to keep allowing Nolan access to them both if he was going to abandon them like he might have done already with his own family? Raina had learned the hard way, time and time again, what abandonment felt like, how much it hurt. Could she even consider risking that for JJ? He was still so young. Still so reliant on her to protect him.

And what of Nolan's wife? Was she someone Raina had met before? Someone she came across in her day-to-day life? She hated the thought that for some poor soul she might become the other woman.

Her mind was whirling with so many worries that she barely noticed the pageant was up to the final number. The children were singing "Silent Night" and the audience had joined in. Beside her, the sound of Nolan's tenor forced her attention back to the present. Sometimes, she reminded herself, you simply had to let go and let God. Maybe it really was as simple as that.

She felt herself begin to relax a little as she joined in for the final lines of the carol. But then a jarring thought sideswiped her. For all her ponderings she hadn't stopped to consider the situation with Jeb or the very large sum of money she had in her purse right now.

With the pageant over, people began to rise from their seats and jostle one another on the way to the main doors. Raina felt Nolan's hand at her elbow, steadying her in the crush as they filed out of their row of seats. Raina turned to him.

"I have to go out the back and collect JJ. Please don't rush off. I know he's going to want to see you."

"And you? Do you want to see me?" Nolan asked, pulling Raina to one side so the crowd could eddy past them without bumping them again.

"I'll be honest—I really don't know. Part of me says, yes, but—"

"I understand. If you'd rather, you can make my apologies to JJ."

She could see the hurt in his eyes, watched the light in them dim a little. It made up her mind.

"Come back to our house for a hot chocolate with JJ. He's going to take some time to unwind before getting off to bed tonight anyway."

Nolan looked at her and she saw the slight curl at the edges of his lips. "Are you sure? I understand if you—"

"No." It was her turn to interrupt him. "I'm sure. Look, he's waiting. I'll see you back at the house, okay?"

"I'll wait for you in the parking lot," Nolan said in a voice that brooked no argument. "And I'll follow you home."

Knowing he'd be there, waiting in the darkness outside, made Raina feel warm inside. And when Jeb showed up for his money, either outside the hall or later, back at her house, she'd deal with it then. Actually, thinking about it, having Nolan handy might make the whole process go more smoothly. She doubted Jeb would try anything stupid with another person there.

"Okay, that's good of you. Thank you."

Later, with JJ in tow and wrapped up again in his winter coat and beanie, they walked quickly to the car. As good as his word, Nolan had pulled up his SUV alongside hers and was waiting in the frigid air.

"Did you see me, No'an?" JJ asked excitedly as they approached the car.

"I did, champ. You were great."

Her little boy's smile made Raina glad she'd asked Nolan back to the house. JJ had had enough of her short-tempered company this week. Goodness only knew, if Nolan hadn't been there tonight, she wouldn't have thought twice about taking JJ home—no doubt kicking and screaming—over the costume issue.

She looked around the parking lot for Jeb. But among all the families loading their preschoolers into their cars and saying bye to their friends, there was no sign of him. Maybe he'd turn up at the house, she decided as she drove along the road toward home. She flicked her eyes to the rearview mirror, reassured by the sight of Nolan's vehicle following her at a safe distance. She was all over the place as far as he was concerned. If only she could trust her heart and they could discover exactly where this complicated relationship of theirs could go. But she'd trusted her heart before and look where that had landed her. She didn't want to ever go through that again.

At the house, Nolan offered to supervise JJ as he changed into his pajamas while she made the hot chocolate. Raina gratefully accepted. As she heated milk on her stove she could hear JJ's excited tones tempered by Nolan's calmer deeper voice down the hall and closed her eyes for just a moment, wondering what it might be like if this were to become a regular, even daily event. How did that make her feel?

A commotion at the kitchen door made her turn as she started to fill the mugs. Nolan had given JJ a piggyback ride from his bedroom and the two of them were laughing. Raina couldn't help but join in.

"Who wants marshmallows?" she asked as she finished pouring the hot drinks.

"Me!" JJ crowed from his perch. "And No'an, too."

Raina looked to Nolan for confirmation. "Are you a marshmallow man?"

"Through and through," he said.

His word were simple at face value but she found herself left wondering if he'd meant more by that. She had to stop overthinking everything. It was time to just let some things find their natural course. She dropped marshmallows in each of the mugs and put them on a tray to carry through to the sitting room.

"Let me take that for you," Nolan offered, swinging JJ down to the floor.

"Thanks."

Raina followed Nolan and JJ and relished just how good it felt to share something as simple as carrying a tray, rather than being responsible for everything herself. But even so, she couldn't allow herself to simply give in to the comfort of this moment. Nolan still had secrets and until he was prepared to share them with her, she had to guard her heart.

Even as she thought it, she knew it was too late. Her heart was already a lost cause when it came to this man. Had been from the moment he'd kissed her. It was why discovering his subterfuge had been so painful.

She watched from the door as Nolan encouraged JJ to kneel on the floor by the coffee table to sip his drink. Obviously sensing her scrutiny, he looked up.

"You okay?" he asked.

She smiled and nodded. "I think so," she answered, and stepped forward to accept the mug he held out for her.

It wasn't long before JJ was drooping with exhaustion. To Raina's surprise he made no argument when she said it was bedtime. He asked to be carried to bed and she lifted him comfortably into her arms and held him close as she went down the hallway to his room. It was a constant marvel to her that this growing child had come from her body. A marvel and a precious gift.

So much responsibility came with parenthood. She had to be certain she was making the right decisions for herself, sure, but for JJ most of all. He deserved only the very best in life. Did that include a second chance with Nolan? she wondered as she supervised JJ brushing his teeth and then carried him to his bed.

JJ was out like a light before she'd even made it to his bedroom. She left the door ajar for him so the nightlight in the hallway could provide enough light should he stir, and she walked slowly back toward the living room. Nolan was sitting on the couch, his mug on the table in front of him.

"Your hot chocolate is cold," he commented. "Can I reheat it for you?"

She shook her head. "It's okay, I'm used to that."

A distant look passed through his eyes as he nodded and gave a short laugh. "Yeah, I bet. Seems that when you have kids nothing is ever eaten or drunk hot or chilled, right? Room temperature is your best friend."

Was he talking about his own child, his own life? He seemed to understand what it was like. Raina couldn't speak for fear that she'd just come straight out and ask him about the little she'd overheard about his wife and kid, but a sense of self-preservation made her hold her tongue. She wasn't even sure that she wanted to know. She knew that made her sound selfish, at least in her own mind.

She drank her lukewarm chocolate and let Nolan steer the conversation to a review of the evening's performance. And while she laughed and talked and agreed with him, she found herself thinking how very much she wished this kind of evening could become a regular event for them. She looked at the clock, startled to see that another full hour had passed since she'd put JJ to bed.

Nolan followed her gaze and made an exclamation. "I'm sorry, I'm keeping you up."

Raina felt a flush of heat and awareness suffuse her body, along with a longing that when she went to bed, they could go together. She shoved the thought to the back of her mind. It was ridiculous. She needed to get her crazy hormones under control. Desire was clouding rationality, and it was that very rationality that got her through every day without falling apart. If she lost that, where would she be?

"Thanks for coming tonight," she said, standing up and putting the mugs on the tray to return them to the kitchen.

Nolan stood also and reached once more for the tray. His fingers brushed hers and her already jangling nerves surged to awareness, making her jerk the tray away.

"It's okay, I can manage," she insisted before turning away from him before he could see the rush of color that stained her cheeks.

Raina set the tray down on the kitchen counter and looked at her reflection in the dark window above. This was ridiculous. She'd barely seen him in the past week and a half and now she was a jittering mass of contradictions in his company. She'd told herself she was better off without him, that she didn't need a man like him in her life, but no matter what her head said, her body told a different story. Even now her breathing was slightly ragged and she felt aware of every brush of her clothing over her sensitized skin. If this was how she reacted when he did nothing more than touch her with a fingertip, she'd be a complete and utter mess if they went any further.

"Raina? You okay? I'm heading off now. Thanks for the drink."

She took a steadying breath and went back to the sitting room.

"You're welcome and thanks again for defusing that

situation with JJ before the pageant. I couldn't have done that without you."

"Only too happy to help out."

He walked toward the door and Raina followed. In the entranceway he paused a moment and then turned to face her.

"Raina, I meant what I said to you earlier tonight. Can I hope that you'll give me another chance to prove to you that I'm not all bad?"

Raina gave him a twisted smile. "I don't have a particularly good track record with bad men."

He smiled back in return but she could see the hurt in his eyes. The knowledge that she was categorizing him with the other deadbeats she'd fallen for in the past.

"Then let's set the record straight, together," he murmured and leaned forward.

She hadn't known he was going to kiss her, at least not consciously. But while her mind may have been slow on the uptake, her body certainly wasn't. She leaned into him, meeting him more than halfway and closing the gap between them. His arms wrapped around her, one hand lifting to spread through her hair.

The second his lips touched hers, she knew she was lost. What was life for if you couldn't take second chances? His lips upon hers were electric, sending a pulse of longing through her body that made her tremble in response. He tasted of hot chocolate and more. Of something darker, spicier, deeper and more forbidden. Logic told her she should pull back, end this. End all of it. But logic took a backseat to the sensation and the promise that poured through her body at this gentlest of caresses.

Raina raised her hands to Nolan's chest. Was it a subconscious attempt to keep some barrier between them, or was it so she could feel the hard strength of his lean muscles beneath the finely woven cotton of his shirt? Her hands tingled as she touched him, as her fingers spread out and her palms soaked up his heat. She ached to feel his skin, to touch him all over, but she daren't ask him to stay. It was too soon. Too much. And she still had far too many questions.

When Nolan pulled back and let his hands drop away from her, Raina felt physically bereft.

"I'll call you tomorrow, okay?" he said, stepping away and opening the front door.

Words failing her, Raina could only nod. After he'd closed the door behind him she stood there for several minutes, the fingertips of one hand pressed to her lips as if she could hold on to the moment—the sweetness, the promise—they'd just shared. But, like everything good in her life, the sensation was a fleeting one, gone before she heard his car start up outside and pull away from the curb.

She wanted him. She knew that. Acknowledged it with an honesty that brought tears to her eyes. But could she have him? Dare she?

Only time would tell.

Thirteen

If the staff at the sheriff's office thought that Nolan looked like someone who'd pulled an all-nighter then that's probably because he had. When he caught sight of his reflection in the outer doors, the red eyes and scruffy jaw, he grimaced. Certainly not his usual *GQ*-style appearance but then it wouldn't be the first time Nolan had looked a bit frayed around the edges.

He'd never felt quite as invested in the result of his work as he had with what he'd done last night. The work itself, and his reasons for doing it, had made one thing abundantly clear to him. He wasn't falling in love with Raina Patterson. He was already there. He loved her. There was no question about it. Yes, it was fast; yes, it had surprised him; and, yes, he'd fought it. But it's what had kept him going at about two this morning when he was questioning his sanity in finding out all there was to know about Jeb Pickering.

Raina was his reason for being here—both at the sheriff's office and in Royal altogether. While his work had sent him here, she was what would keep him. He only needed to convince her of that fact. A cakewalk, right? He snorted under his breath and earned a stern glance from a passing deputy.

"Can I help you, sir?" a woman behind the front counter asked.

"Yes, I know I don't have an appointment but I need to see the sheriff, if he's in. It's urgent."

"Just about every man coming in to see the sheriff says the same thing," she answered with a roll of her eyes. "Your name?"

Nolan gave it and thought he saw a glimpse of recognition in the woman's eyes.

"Howard Dane's boy?"

He nodded. He might be a grown man but he'd always be his father's son in this town—and proud of it, he realized. "Yes, he's my dad."

The receptionist nodded. "Take a seat over there. I'll see if Sheriff Battle's available."

Nolan sat down on a hard vinyl-covered seat against the wall and drummed his fingers on his leg. He was lucky he didn't have to wait long.

"Nolan Dane?" The sheriff had come out to the reception area himself. "Welcome home."

"Thanks," Nolan answered, rising to his feet and offering his hand.

"What brings you to my office?"

"Can we talk in private?"

"Sure, c'mon back."

Once they were seated in a private room, Nolan didn't waste any time.

"I have information on a man named Jeb Pickering. He's got a long list of convictions for petty crime but right now he's wanted in New Mexico on third-degree felony charges."

"Tell me more," Sheriff Battle said, leaning forward with his elbows on the desk between them.

"He's the ex-partner of Raina Patterson, who runs Priceless out at the Courtyard."

The sheriff nodded. "Yeah, I know her. Lost her store in town in the tornado. Brave woman. Has a little boy. He'd be about three now, I guess."

Nolan was impressed that the man could recall one of the people of Royal so easily, but then again that's probably why Nate Battle was reelected each term. He cared. Nolan was counting on that to help him rid Raina of Jeb's shadow forever.

"That's the one. Pickering skipped out on her but keeps coming back for handouts. Seems he has a bit of trouble with gambling and drinking."

"Not the best of combinations but not necessarily a crime, unfortunately."

"No," Nolan agreed. "However, we can now add manslaughter while driving under the influence of alcohol and skipping bail to his list of charms."

The sheriff let out a low whistle. "I see. And you know this how?"

Nolan quickly explained, showing the sheriff the information he'd gathered. After reading it carefully, the sheriff looked up.

"D'you know where he is now?"

"Not exactly, but I know where he'll be tonight."

The anger he was feeling at Jeb Pickering's callous disregard of life added cold hard inflection to his words as Nolan outlined his confrontation with Pickering last night.

"So he thinks you'll be there to give him money so he can head on his way out of state again." The sheriff nodded. "I think we can work with you."

"I was hoping you'd say that." Nolan smiled and leaned back in his chair.

"Give me the details and I'll get a couple of my men together, and I'll alert the New Mexico authorities that their chicken will be coming home to roost."

Nolan stamped his feet against the cold as he waited in the parking area for Jeb to show. So far Nolan hadn't seen a sign of anyone, although he had every confidence that Nate Battle and his men were nearby.

The skitter of a stone on the pavement made Nolan turn around.

"Pickering," he acknowledged as the man slipped out from the shadows.

"You got my money?"

Nolan ignored his request. "I've been doing a bit of research on you, man. It seems you're a wanted criminal."

Jeb's face turned nasty. "What the hell do you know? I've been doing a bit of research of my own. You're just some fancy-pants lawyer who couldn't even keep his wife and son alive. Now give me my money," he demanded as he yanked one hand from his pocket and shoved it in Nolan's direction.

Nolan fought to ignore the man's gibe but even so, it cut deep. The truth always did. He forced himself to focus—to do what was right for Raina. Yes, he might not have been able to save Bennett and Carole, but he'd be damned if he ever saw another person he loved hurt when he could do something about it.

He took a step closer to Jeb. "Turn yourself in, man. You know the authorities are going to catch up with you sooner or later."

"Not if I get to Mexico they won't. With that money I reckon I can disappear for a while."

"Oh, you'll disappear for a while, all right," Nolan

agreed as he spied Nate Battle and a couple of his deputies move silently up behind Jeb.

Jeb grinned, but then he realized that Nolan's words had held a double entendre. "Whaddya mean?"

"I mean there is no money. Not from me and not from Raina either."

Jeb started to swear and launched himself forward at Nolan, both fists now swinging in fury. Nate and his deputies closed the distance between them and wrestled him to the ground, but not before a punch caught the edge of Nolan's jaw making his head snap back. But one shot was all the other man got and it was with a great deal of satisfaction that Nolan watched the deputies cuff Jeb and haul him to his feet to read him his rights then lead him to their car—as he loudly and energetically protested the whole way.

"I think we can add resisting arrest to his list of charges, don't you?" Nate Battle commented as he straightened his jacket.

"Yeah," Nolan said, rubbing his fingers along his jaw where Jeb's fist had connected.

"You want to press charges for that?"

"No." Nolan shook his head. "I'm pretty sure he has enough charges against him now to ensure that he won't bother Raina again."

The sheriff gave him a piercing look. "Like that is it? You're soft on Raina Patterson?"

Nolan nodded.

Nate reached out a hand to Nolan. "As I said this morning, good to have you back in Royal."

Nolan shook the sheriff's hand. "Thanks. It really is good to be back."

"I guess we'll be seeing more of you."

"If you mean, am I staying in town, the answer is yes. And I'm rejoining dad's practice, too."

"That's good. We need men like you and your dad fighting for the vulnerable people in this town."

With that, Nate tipped his hat and turned and walked toward his car.

Nolan stood there in the darkness, oblivious now to the cold that whipped around him. Home. He really was home again and he had the approval of the sheriff. It probably didn't get much better than that in terms of acceptance. There was just one more obstacle to overcome. Raina. He'd taken care of her past, now he needed to share his own. And for the life of him, he didn't know how he was supposed to do this right.

Raina checked the floor safe in the shop for the umpteenth time to reassure herself the money she was holding for Jeb was still there. Well, where else would it be? She closed the door and spun the dial before pulling the trap door down over it again. It had been a couple of days since she'd promised him she'd have the money ready. It wasn't like him not to show and the waiting was making her jumpy.

Even his phone calls and texts had stopped. So what on earth had happened to him? She didn't dare hope that he'd left and forgotten all about it. That wasn't his style at all.

Raina got to her feet and went over to the cheval mirror she had propped in the corner of her small office and checked her appearance. Nolan was picking her up soon and taking her out for dinner. Her dad had JJ at his place for one of their much anticipated Saturday nights together and for some stupid reason Raina felt more nervous about tonight than she had on her very first date with a boy.

This is Nolan, she kept telling herself. *You know him. You trust him...mostly.* She shook her head. She trusted him, she just didn't know everything she needed to know about him yet. There was a difference. Of course he had secrets, so did she, didn't she? She sighed. Maybe that was her trouble. She trusted too darn easily.

She studied her reflection in the mirror. The long floral skirt she'd teamed with a pair of high black boots made her feel feminine and pretty, although after a day on her feet, her toes were beginning to complain. It'd be worth it, she'd told herself as she examined her reflection and smoothed the soft sweater she'd chosen over her hips. She didn't often wear black but the contrast between the sweater and her creamy skin brought out the light in her eyes. Noticing her makeup could definitely do with a touch-up, she grabbed her makeup bag from her purse and made a few running repairs, eager to look her best for the man who continued to send her pulse flying.

The bell chimed out front and she quickly shoved her makeup bag back into her purse and went out into the shop, a smile already stretching her lips.

"Nolan, you're early!" she exclaimed.

"Would it sound ridiculous if I said I couldn't wait to see you?"

He bent and kissed her cheek and even though the touch was about as innocent as you could get, Raina immediately felt her body flare to aching life. She wanted him so much and it was quite clear to her that he felt the same way.

But why didn't he tell her about his wife and son?

Oh, sure, she could come right out and ask him, but she strongly felt that this was Nolan's story to tell on his own terms—even if waiting didn't sit comfortably with her. She'd learned the hard way not to push a man for the truth. In the past, and with Jeb in particular, men had only told her what they thought she wanted to hear. She didn't want to travel down that road with Nolan. He'd tell her about his family when he was ready, she reminded herself for the umpteenth time.

She pushed the niggling thoughts to the back of her mind, determined to enjoy his company tonight.

"I've been looking forward to tonight, too."

"Is there anything I can do to help you lock up?" Nolan asked.

"No, I'm just about finished. It's been quiet today. I guess not everyone wants to buy antiques for Christmas."

"I'd say that was a shame but if it means we get to spend more time together, who am I to complain?"

Nolan smiled at her but Raina's attention was caught by a dark bruise on the edge of his jaw. She raised a hand and gently touched the mark with her fingertips.

"What on earth have you been up to to get this?" she asked.

Nolan grabbed her hand and kissed her fingertips before letting it go again. "It's nothing. Something just flew up and hit me when I wasn't expecting it."

She searched his face, but he just smiled at her in return.

"Are you ready to go? We can get a drink before the movies if we leave now."

"Sure," she shrugged. "I doubt I'll get any last-minute customers at this stage of the day."

Raina grabbed her jacket and set the alarm system before they left through the front door. She shivered as the cold air outside cut through her.

"It almost feels as if it could snow," she commented as Nolan held open his car door for her and helped her up into the SUV.

"Yeah, it might. But even if it does, I doubt it'll stick. You know what it's like around here this time of year."

They made small talk in the car, mostly discussing JJ and how excited he was about Christmas being only six days away. Nolan was good company, the best male company she'd ever had, she decided. If only he'd open up about his past.

The movie was a comedy, and Raina was glad because she loved to hear Nolan laugh—which he did, loudly and often. Afterward, they walked to a nearby Italian place she'd never been to before. The proprietors greeted Nolan like a long lost son and she didn't miss the glance that passed between the Italian couple when Nolan introduced her.

They were shown to a secluded table with low lighting and the ubiquitous red checkered tablecloth and a candle inserted in a used Chianti bottle.

"This is lovely," Raina commented as they studied their menus. "Do you come here often?"

"Not in a long time," he admitted. "It used to be a favorite."

A favorite with his wife perhaps? Maybe that explained the owners' slightly uncomfortable expressions when he'd introduced her.

"So, can you recommend anything?"

"Let's see," Nolan drawled, running his eyes across the menu card. "The veal scalloppini is always good, especially if you're not crazy about pasta. Hell, I didn't think. You do like Italian food, don't you? I just assumed—"

"I love Italian food, and the scalloppini sounds perfect," she hastened to reassure him.

"Okay. What about an appetizer?" he prompted.

"You choose. I'm pretty much okay with everything."

He nodded and beckoned the waiter over, ordering them a platter of antipasto to start, followed by the veal and a bottle of Chianti to go with it.

Raina was feeling decidedly mellow by the end of the evening. The movie, the food and the company had all been incredible, and when Nolan drove back to her house she knew what her next step was.

"Will you come inside?" she asked as they sat in the car in the pitch-dark night.

"I'd like that," Nolan agreed, and together they walked up the front path to her house.

Inside, she hung their coats up and led him to the sitting room. Her heart was beating double time. She knew what she wanted, but was it what he wanted, too?

"Did you want a nightcap, or a coffee?"

Nolan only shook his head and reached for her, pulling her into his arms. "No, I only want you."

"Then we're in agreement," she said softly, feeling a run of excitement deep inside. "Because I want you, too."

She cupped his face and pulled it down to hers and kissed him with all the pent-up longing she'd harbored since their kiss on Thursday night. Instantly her body leaped to life, her nipples tightening into hard nubs and her breasts growing full and heavy. She pressed against his chest, as if that could somehow ease the aching demand, but instead it only heightened it.

Nolan's hands splayed across her back, holding her to him as if they could be molded together forever. One hand drifted to her lower back and pulled her body more firmly against his. The hard ridge of his arousal pressed against her, sending a thrill of anticipation throughout her entire body and ending in a pulse of longing that centered at her core.

"I want to touch you," she whispered against his mouth. "All of you."

She tugged at his shirt, pulling it from the waistband of his trousers and pushing her hands underneath. His skin was smooth and hot, and he shuddered at her touch. Raina forced herself to draw away slightly so she could work his buttons loose. Eventually she succeeded and she pushed the fabric wide open, exposing his tanned skin. A light dusting of hair peppered his chest before narrowing in a tempting path down his abdomen and lower. She traced that line with her fingers and felt his stomach muscles contract beneath her touch.

"Raina, I—"

Whatever he'd been about to say was lost as she leaned forward and pressed her lips to one nipple, her tongue swirling around the smooth disc and teasing its tip into a taut bud. She raked her nails lightly across the other, eliciting a groan of need from deep inside him. The sound gave her a sense of power and she took her time exploring his upper body with her hands, her mouth, her tongue. When Nolan pulled her up to kiss him again, she was one hot mess of need, and when his hands drifted to the waistband of her top she didn't hesitate to let him remove it for her.

Nolan backed her toward the couch and gently guided her down before joining her there. He held himself up on one elbow as he traced the lacy cup of her bra. His eyes looked darker than usual, his pupils almost consuming the brown of his irises, and a light flush of color stained his cheekbones.

"You are so beautiful," he murmured before leaning down and tracing a line in the valley of her breasts with his tongue.

It was what she wanted and yet it still wasn't enough. Raina squirmed against him, desperate to ease the insistent demand of her body. Nolan reached behind her, unsnapped the clasp of her bra and gently tugged the garment away from her before dropping it to the carpet.

For a moment Raina felt self-conscious. She had stretch marks all over her body, silvered now, but a continuing reminder of the son she'd borne. But her insecurity soon vanished as Nolan paid homage to her breasts, teasing first one tip, then the other, with his mouth and tongue. As he drew one into his mouth and suckled hard, she felt a spear of pleasure drive through her body, almost sending her over the edge. She'd never felt so responsive.

She murmured his name as he worked his way down, tracing the lines of her rib cage with his strong fingers and following each touch with a kiss, a lick, a suck of his mouth. Her nerves were screaming for more and she squirmed under his sensual assault. She'd never felt this much before. Never wanted another human being like she wanted him.

Her body felt empty, demanding to be filled, to be led to the precipice of the pleasure she knew she'd find under his touch. Nolan pulled away and she made a sound of protest, which he silenced with a swift kiss.

"Just making you more comfortable," he said, and then he reached for her boots.

He undid first one, then the other, easing them off her feet and peeling away her stockings and tossing them to the floor to join her top and her bra. When Nolan reached for the fastening on the side of her skirt and eased the zipper down, she lifted her hips, allowing him to slide the garment off.

Dressed only in her panties, she was assailed by a sense of awkwardness and moved her hands in an attempt to cover herself. Nolan merely caught her wrists in gentle fingers and pulled her hands away.

"Don't," he admonished. "I meant what I said before. You're beautiful. Every. Inch. Of you." He punctuated his words with a kiss on her belly. Her hips. The edge of her panties.

Raina let her head drop back against the arm of the couch and closed her eyes, giving herself over to the delicious sensations that poured through her. One moment Nolan's hands and mouth were at the edge of her panties and the next her panties were gone and she could feel the heat of his breath against the soft skin of her inner thighs.

He pressed a wet kiss against her skin, and then blew out cool air. She shivered as anticipation threatened to destroy her mind even as her body coiled in hope and eagerness, awaiting his next touch. She wasn't disappointed. His fingers traced a delicious line from her hip to her groin and back again before moving ever so slowly lower.

She knew she was wet and ready for him and yet when his fingers parted her outer lips and traced the entrance of her body she almost jolted right up off the couch.

"Too much?" he asked softly.

"No, not too much. Never too much," she gasped.

She forced herself to relax and let her thighs fall open, giving him easier access to the secrets of her body. When he eased one finger inside her she murmured her approval and clenched against him involuntarily, sending delight spiraling outward from where he touched.

"You feel so good," Nolan said, his voice growing huskier by the minute.

"You make me feel so much," Raina countered breathlessly.

She could feel her climax hovering just on the periphery and knew, without a doubt, that it wouldn't take much more to send her on a trajectory of pleasure that would shatter her into a million pieces. Nolan eased his finger from her body and then reentered her with two. She loved the sense of fullness it gave her, and as he brushed against that magical part of her, she felt the first pull of orgasm.

Her last rational thought was of his mouth closing over her, of his tongue rolling around the tight bead of nerve endings at her center and of the draw of his mouth as he pushed her gently over the edge and tumbling headlong into bliss.

Nolan gathered her into his arms as the final waves of satisfaction petered away into lassitude, and he lifted her off the couch. She made no protest as he carried her down the hallway and deposited her in her bed, but it wasn't until he pulled the comforter up over her naked body that she realized he didn't intend to join her there, or stay.

"Nolan?" she asked, reaching out for him. "We haven't finished."

He bent and pressed his lips to hers. "We have—for tonight."

"But you… I…" She was lost for words to describe the imbalance of what had happened.

"It's okay. Now sleep. Tomorrow's another day. I'll let myself out."

This wasn't how she'd imagined things ending tonight at all, Raina thought as she lay in the darkness and heard the front door close, shortly followed by the sound of Nolan's car driving away. And, while her body was sated, she still felt as though an essential ingredient was missing. She reached across the vacant expanse of her bed and realized that she already missed him. And still she didn't have the truth.

Fourteen

Raina spent the next few days in a blur of confusion about her feelings for Nolan. Their evening together had been wonderful, truly so. And he'd made her feel cherished and special and all those things that she'd decided, after Jeb, were nonnegotiable. But high on her list was honesty, too. Was withholding things about himself the same as being dishonest? She began to worry that the longer it took, the less likely it was she was going to hear about his past from him. And Raina knew she didn't want to hear it from anyone else.

Even so, it didn't stop her from looking forward to seeing him as she had at lunch on Monday, and then for a quick coffee yesterday afternoon. Her father had cautioned her about rushing into things too fast, with a reminder about where that had left her the last time, and she'd acknowledged his concerns. After all, hadn't he been the one to stand by her through all the fallout from each previous disastrous relationship?

The thought brought her back to Jeb. There had still been no contact from him and when she attempted to call his cell phone, it was disconnected.

At least there were still some things in her life she kept a handle on. She smiled to herself as she adjusted the Christmas display in her store window. The antique Santa and the child's sled had garnered a great deal of comment from passersby, bringing them into the store and boosting her small-ticket item sales quite comfortably. And the sled itself had sold, too—with the new owner planning to pick it up before New Year's Eve.

All in all, her December sales had been very strong. Factoring in the success of her craft lessons, things were definitely looking up for the New Year. Which reminded her, she needed to finalize the newsletter she'd be sending out with the new classes and timetables for January.

Outside the store, a car pulled up in the parking area and Raina noticed a young woman alight. She recognized the petite blonde instantly—Clare Connelly. Raina waved as Clare started to walk toward Priceless.

"Good morning," Raina said with a welcoming smile as she opened the door for her. "Have a day off?"

Clare's role as chief pediatric nurse at Royal Memorial Hospital kept her very busy but if anyone could handle busyness with a liberal dose of chaos, it was Clare. Her no-nonsense approach to her work was well-known around Royal and she held the respect of everyone who'd had babies under her care.

"I'm on a late shift tonight but I needed to get some last-minute Christmas shopping done. I need something special for my elderly neighbor. She's such a darling."

"Does she collect anything in particular?" Raina asked as they walked deeper into the store.

Clare wrinkled her brow in concentration. "Not anything specific. Do you mind if I look around for a bit? I'm not 100 percent sure of what I want but I'm hoping I'll recognize what I'm looking for when I see it."

"Sure," Raina said with a smile. "Holler if you need me. I'll just be out back, okay?"

"Thanks," Clare answered as she turned away with a distracted look on her face.

It wasn't like Clare to be indecisive, Raina thought as she pottered around in the back of the store, wielding her dusting cloth and giving some of the larger pieces of furniture a rub with furniture oil. After a few minutes, she looked up at Clare, who'd barely moved from where she left her. The other woman was staring blankly at a Royal Albert tea set as if she was waiting for some genie to waft out of the teapot's spout or something.

Raina worked her way back toward Clare.

"Are you sure I can't help you find something?"

Clare started and gasped in surprise. "Oh, I'm sorry. I was a million miles away. Yes," she said on a sigh. "I would be glad of your help. I know my neighbor has a thimble collection that she's added to ever since she was a little girl. She used to be quite skillful with a needle and thread from what I understand, and most of the thimbles are well used, but her eyesight's deteriorated as she's grown older, and she's developed arthritis and can't work with her hands anymore."

"That's a shame," Raina sympathized. "We have some beautiful handcrafted lace and linen doilies here from the early 1900s. Do you think she'd be interested in them?"

"They sound gorgeous. Show me."

Raina brought Clare over to a large mahogany sideboard and glass-fronted hutch that she used to showcase several of her better pieces of china. She slid open a drawer and removed a tissue-wrapped package. Her hand shook a little as she remembered the last time she'd handled the doilies, and how she'd almost used one to mop ice cream off the front of Nolan's trousers. A smile curved her lips at the memory. How much further had they come since then? Raina unwrapped the tissue and spread the doilies on the gleaming wooden surface of the sideboard.

"They're rather beautiful, don't you think?"

Each one had a round, finely woven linen center and a painstakingly created lace edge. There were four in total, each one slightly different in pattern from the other but with a floral theme that took Raina's breath away every time she looked at them. Such craftsmanship, such patience. She envied the woman who'd created them because she doubted she would ever have been able to have produced such exquisite work.

"They're gorgeous! And they're perfect. Thank you. I should have known you'd find exactly what I needed," Clare said on a note of relief.

"It's my job to make sure you do." Raina smiled back at her. "Clare, I hope you don't mind me saying this, but you don't seem yourself. Is everything okay?"

"Oh, it's nothing in particular. I'm just really stressed with the reorganization of the neonatal unit at the hospital. I'm sure the pressure will drop a little once the new wing is open next month. It's been a tough year."

Raina nodded. "But we're getting through it."

Clare looked at her and smiled. "Yes, we are. We're nothing if not determined, right?"

Raina smiled back. "Would you like me to gift wrap the doilies for you?"

"Would you? That would save me the bother, thank you."

"Come on over to the counter...unless you'd like to keep browsing?"

"Maybe I'll come in some other time and have a good poke around. Perhaps a day when I'm a bit less distracted," Clare laughed.

"Good idea," Raina agreed and walked over to the counter where she rewrapped the doilies in fresh tissue and put them in a gold box that she covered in a vibrant Christmas paper. "There you are," she said as she finished tying a red bow around the box.

"That looks far better than anything I would have done," Clare said admiringly.

"I get a bit more practice. I'm sure you can still diaper and swaddle a baby faster and more effectively than I ever could."

"You could be right," Clare conceded. "How is JJ?"

"He's doing really great, thanks. Of course he can barely sleep for counting the nights until Christmas."

"Good thing there are only two more to go."

"For my sake as well as JJ's," Raina agreed vehemently.

A thought occurred to Raina. She knew Clare was about the same age as Nolan and probably went to the local high school at around the same time as he would have. She'd told herself she wouldn't probe into his past, but with the opportunity presenting itself, maybe it was time she did a little poking around.

"Say, do you remember Nolan Dane?"

"Nolan? Yeah, sure. Why?"

"You know he was working on behalf of Samson Oil, don't you?"

Clare's mouth twisted into moue of distaste. "Yeah, I know. Seems like Royal is evenly divided about whether Samson Oil is a good thing or not."

Raina nodded. "I know. But he resigned from that position. He's going back to family law."

Clare's face brightened. "Is he? That's great. I know everyone around here was so shocked when he left. Of course, it was totally understandable after what he'd been through but no one really expected him to leave. He'd always been so woven into the fabric of Royal, y'know? Excelled at high school—popular and great at sports. It didn't matter what he put his hand to, he did it brilliantly. Our Nolan was quite the golden boy but never arrogant about it. Everyone liked him."

"What he'd been through?" Raina prompted, even though her stomach curled at what she might be told. Being nosy like this was wrong on so many levels—what if she didn't like what she heard? Raina forced herself to clear her mind of anxiety. Yes, this was Nolan's tale to tell, but to be honest, she was done with waiting. She wanted to know. And she'd have to take whatever she heard and deal with it.

"Oh, you don't know, do you? I keep forgetting that you didn't grow up here. That's a compliment by the way," Clare said with a warm smile. "Like I said, Nolan was always a high achiever but so was Carole, his high school sweetheart. They went to college together and then on to law school. Once they got their degrees they came back to Royal and married, and a year later they had a little boy, Bennett. Nolan and Carole were the couple everyone wanted to emulate. They were successful, sure, but they were also so in love. You couldn't look at them without feeling it."

Raina felt each one of Clare's words as if it was a physical blow but she tried hard not to linger on the pain. He'd had a life before she'd met him. So what on earth had gone wrong?

Clare continued, oblivious to the turmoil Raina was going through. "Carole returned to work soon after Bennett was born and I think he was about eighteen months old when it happened."

Raina hesitated to ask but couldn't help herself. "What happened?"

"It was awful. Apparently Nolan used to take Bennett to day care each morning as part of their routine. This particular day he heard that one of his clients had been severely beaten by her husband the night before. She called and asked him to come into the hospital to see her early, so he did. Of course that meant that Carole had to take Bennett to day care. Trouble was, she was in the middle of some really important negotiations her firm was handling at the same time and apparently she got paged while she was driving. She called her office and completely forgot Bennett was in the back of her car. They think he'd probably fallen asleep, too. Carole drove straight to her office and went to work. It was July and her car was parked in direct sunlight. Bennett died of heat exhaustion."

Raina gasped in horror. She'd heard of forgotten baby syndrome and, while she'd never understood it, she could only imagine how unbelievably awful it would be to have it happen to you.

"Did no one at the day care call to see where the baby was?" she asked.

"Apparently they had a new staff member on and they failed to figure it out at first. It wasn't until lunchtime that someone mentioned him. By then it was too late. Of course, the police were sympathetic but they had to bring charges of manslaughter and felony child abuse. It was just an awful time and it divided a lot of the people here.

"Poor Carole, she couldn't live with what she'd done. Before their case even got to court she took her life. Six months after that Nolan was gone, too—to LA, where he's been ever since."

"No wonder he didn't come back," Raina sympathized. "It must have been awful for him to lose them both."

Clare nodded. "It was a sad time for everyone who knew them but, of course, most of all for him."

The old grandfather clock near the front door chimed the hour and Clare glanced at it in consternation.

"Oh, heck, is that the time? I really need to get going. Thanks so much for the help with the Christmas gift,

Raina. I really appreciate it." She cocked her head and looked at Raina with a funny expression on her face. "You know, you actually look a bit like Carole. Same coloring and similar features. You could almost have passed for sisters. She was beautiful, too. Thanks again!"

Clare was gone in a whirlwind of movement, leaving Raina alone with her thoughts. Her heart ached for Nolan's loss. She didn't even want to begin to imagine what it would be like to lose JJ; just thinking about it was enough to bring tears to her eyes. But hearing Nolan's story brought a lot of things into sharper focus. Like his confidence and ability with her son and his patience. Those were all characteristics of someone who was used to being with a child.

She could almost understand him keeping his past to himself, but for one thing—her similarity to his late and obviously much beloved wife. Was that why he thought he was falling in love with *her*? Was it simply that she and JJ represented all that he'd lost? Were they merely substitutes for the wife and son that had been torn so tragically from his life?

It was impossible to know for sure, at least until he really talked to her. But how could she encourage him to do that? And what would she do if her fears were well-founded? Could she turn him away? It would break her heart if she did, and wouldn't she be breaking his all over again, too? He'd already lost his wife and son. But, she asked herself, could she live her life with him, knowing that he didn't love her for herself, but instead loved her for what she represented to him?

She'd promised herself to never again put herself last in a relationship—that things needed to be on an equal footing or no footing at all. She wouldn't settle for being second best. Which left her where, exactly, with Nolan?

Raina groaned out loud and squeezed her eyes shut. What on earth was she going to do?

Nolan walked up the path to Raina's house on Christmas Eve, ready to collect her and JJ to take them to the service at the nearby church. He'd debated with himself, long and hard, before accepting Raina's invitation to go with them. The last time he'd been here in Royal at Christmas, both Carole and Bennett had been alive. Bennett had been a year old and had been a complete handful in church. Not quite walking but active enough to want to be kept busy through the entire service. The memories were still so bittersweet and painful and yet, today at least, thinking about that time didn't bring the searing shaft of pain it used to. He missed them so very much, but he'd learned he needed to move forward with his life a long time ago. The irony that his moving forward had brought him full circle, and back home, wasn't lost on him.

From the other side of the front door, Nolan could hear JJ's excited chatter as he and Raina got ready. After he rapped his knuckles on the door, JJ's excited shout of "No'an!" came through clear as a bell. Nolan felt his lips turn up in a smile that dispelled any of the lingering doubt or sorrow he'd felt about attending the service tonight. He couldn't help but admit it. It was more than nice to be wanted.

And he wanted in return. Raina opened the door wearing a vibrant red wool coat that complemented her fair skin and dark hair perfectly. He took in her appearance and a jolt of lust rocked him. Since he'd left her in her bed last Saturday, he'd been walking around in a state of semiarousal that had tormented and excited him in equal proportions. He'd wanted nothing more than to make love with Raina that night, to stay wrapped in the comfort of her arms and her body through the dark hours and to wake with her in the morning and know that she was his. But he felt their relationship was still so new, so tenuous, that he'd needed to at least try to take things slower. To allow her time to ease into what he hoped would be their future together before taking what he knew would be an almighty step for them both.

Raina had been hurt before, badly. And he'd hurt her, too. He knew it and regretted it with almost every waking thought. So it was up to him to re-earn her respect. To give her space and time to know that she could love him as much as he already knew he loved her. Which, in a nutshell, meant a whole lot of self-denial on his part. Still, he reminded himself, it didn't hurt a man to be prepared. He patted his jacket pocket and felt the small parcel there. He'd carried it around for a couple of days now, debating when would be the right time, keeping it with him always should the opportunity present itself.

"No'an!" JJ launched himself through the front door and off the top step straight into Nolan's arms.

Nolan caught the little boy and swung him in the air, laughing even as Raina chided the boy for not saying hello properly. After whirling a giggling JJ around Nolan tucked him up on one hip and smiled at Raina.

"Good evening. I take it you're both ready?" he said on a laugh.

"As ready as we'll ever be," Raina said and smiled back.

"No'an! Santa's coming tonight!" JJ squealed excitedly.

"So I hear," Nolan replied, giving the little boy his full attention. "Have you been a good boy all year, JJ?"

For a moment JJ's forehead wrinkled in a frown, then his expression smoothed. "Yup!"

"Then I guess tomorrow morning will be a whole lot of fun for you, won't it?"

"Yup." JJ leaned a little closer to Nolan and cupped a small hand in front of Nolan's ear. "Mommy has a present for you," he whispered loudly. "It's a secret."

Nolan looked at Raina, who was rolling her eyes.

"JJ Patterson, what did I tell you about secrets?"

"That you're not suppos'ta tell other people?"

"That's right."

"But No'an's not other people," JJ protested.

Raina's eyes met Nolan's and the look they shared deepened into something else. Something that made Nolan's heart swell on a note of hope.

"No, honey. Nolan's not other people. He's much more than that."

Silence stretched between them. Nolan wished he could do nothing else but kiss Raina right now. Long and hard and deep. He wanted to demand from her what "more than that" meant to her. But he had to satisfy himself with waiting. Down the street, they heard the church bells begin to chime.

"We'd better get going."

He carried JJ toward his SUV but Raina remained on the front path.

"Shouldn't we take my car? I have JJ's seat in there," she said.

Nolan opened the rear door of the SUV and gestured to the new car seat he'd had installed a couple of days ago.

"You bought a car seat?" she asked, her voice incredulous.

"I thought I ought to," he said simply. "Brand-new and ready for a test drive. How about it, champ?" he asked JJ. "You ready to hop in?"

In answer, JJ scrambled into the car seat and waited to be buckled in.

"You want to check he's secure?" Nolan asked Raina,

who was standing on the sidewalk, a bemused expression on her face.

"No, it's okay. I… I trust you."

The words were simple enough in their expression but they meant the world to Nolan. Now he had only to prove to her that she could trust him in all things—not only with her precious son, but with her heart, as well.

The service at the nearby church was well attended and, given that the congregation was primarily young families, it was kept simple and sweet and involved the children for much of it. He didn't miss the pointed glances Raina received from several people when they saw her at his side. The only sign that she'd noticed anything was the faintest of blushes on her cheeks.

But when the service was over, it was the words of one of the older parishioners that really made her blush.

"Raina Patterson, good to see you've seen sense and have found yourself a decent young man," the old woman said as they left the church with JJ holding both their hands between them.

"Mrs. Baker, Merry Christmas to you," Raina replied courteously, but Nolan could see she was embarrassed by the attention. "This is Nolan Dane. You might have heard of his father, Howard Dane?"

The old lady eyed Nolan up and down as if he was a prime cut of meat before smiling and giving him the benefit of the twinkle in her eye. "I remember teaching your father. He was quite the rascal in his day. Are you a rascal, young man?"

Nolan heard Raina's sharp intake of breath and laughed before replying. "Only when absolutely necessary, ma'am."

Mrs. Baker snorted. "Humph. Cheeky. Just like your father." She leaned across and whispered in Raina's ear. "I'd hold on to this one if I was you, young lady. Good men are hard to find."

Raina was clearly speechless and could do no more than nod. Nolan reached down and gave the old lady a kiss on her wrinkled cheek.

"Merry Christmas, Mrs. Baker. I'll pass your regards on to my dad."

"You do that, young man. You do that."

By the time they left the church and headed home, JJ was still wide-awake and more pumped up than ever. As they arrived at Raina's place, she turned to Nolan, her blue eyes troubled.

"I'm sorry about that, back at the church."

"What for? I enjoyed it."

He held her gaze and watched as the concern faded from her face.

"Hot choclik time!" JJ announced from the backseat.

"Are you coming in for a hot drink?" Raina offered.

"Just try and hold me back."

Inside, Raina put on the TV and tuned in to a channel showing Santa's progress from the North Pole. JJ sat and watched the radar blip on the screen as if his life depended on it.

"Straight to bed after your hot chocolate, JJ."

"Can I stay up and see Santa, Mommy. Please? I be good," JJ pleaded.

"Hey, champ, Santa's a bit of a shy guy. He won't come unless you're tucked up in bed and fast asleep," Nolan answered.

"He won't?" JJ's eyes grew huge.

Nolan assumed a solemn expression and shook his head. "Why don't you come up here and sit with me and tell me what you want for Christmas."

Raina threw Nolan a grateful look. "I'll be right back."

Nolan watched her go through to the kitchen, his eyes caught by the gentle sway of her hips as she walked. Her skirt was not so tight as to be indecent, but not so loose as to hide the perfect shape of her either.

"No'an, you listening to me?" JJ's voice broke through his thoughts.

"Sorry, champ. Yep, I'm listening. What did you ask Santa for?"

"I tol' Santa I want one thing more'n anything else."

"And what's that?"

"It's secret," JJ said with a little frown on his forehead. "Can't tell secrets."

"What about if you just whisper it to me. Like you did before."

JJ mulled over Nolan's suggestion and then got up onto his knees and, leaning against Nolan's shoulder, said in his ear. "I aks'd for you to be my daddy."

Nolan's heart skipped a few beats in his chest. As JJ settled back down beside him he put an arm around the little guy's shoulders to give him a hug. His eyes stung with emotion and the enormity of what JJ had just said.

A rattle of mugs on a tray made him realize that Raina had returned to the room and that she'd overheard JJ's wish for Christmas. She was staring at Nolan, her expression a combination of shock and yearning and something else he couldn't quite put his finger on. He wished he could read her better. Wished he could be sure that she wanted the same thing that JJ wanted.

He chose his next words very carefully.

"That's a mighty special wish, JJ. Being a daddy is a very precious gift. You know what precious is?"

JJ shook his head.

"It's something that means everything to you."

"Like Spider-Man?"

"Even more than that," Nolan said with a smile. "I hope you get your wish, champ, but it's a mighty tall order for poor old Santa."

* * *

Raina set the tray down on the table and passed JJ his small mug of hot chocolate and Nolan his larger one. "There you go, guys."

She averted her gaze from the question in Nolan's eyes. It was too soon, she told herself, even though her heart and soul screamed otherwise. And, yes, while there was nothing physically holding them back, there was an emotional minefield between them that still needed to be successfully negotiated. How could she even think about the future when she wasn't sure that Nolan had dealt with the past?

She hadn't been lying earlier this evening when she said she trusted Nolan. He was exactly what Mrs. Baker had said—a good man. But if she was going to commit to him she needed better than good for her and JJ. She wanted all of him—all his scars, all his truths, all his fears as well as his successes. Not just the parts he was willing to share. It had to be everything, or nothing.

She had to be sure he wanted her for herself, not because she reminded him of his dead wife or because JJ gave him back the chance to be a dad when his own son had been so cruelly taken from him. They both deserved more than that. If Nolan could be honest with her, she knew she'd have no further hesitation in giving herself to him with everything she had. Having him in her and JJ's life was a glowing beacon of what their future could be like. Which made the prospect of turning away from it, from Nolan, terrifying in its enormity.

Fifteen

After Raina caught JJ yawning more than once, she hustled the little guy off to bed but he insisted on both Nolan and her tucking him in. It brought tears to her eyes when JJ's little arms wrapped around Nolan's neck and he hugged him tight before snuggling under the covers.

"Sweet dreams, champ," Nolan said gently as he disentangled JJ's arms.

"Love you, No'an" came JJ's sleepy reply.

Raina saw the look of shock on Nolan's face at JJ's words and watched as he smoothed JJ's hair off his forehead and pressed a kiss there.

As she followed Nolan out of the room and down the hall, her mind was in turmoil. It was already too late to protect JJ from heartache if she shut Nolan out of their lives. And did she even want to do that?

"I've got something for JJ in the car. Do you mind if I put it under the tree for him for tomorrow?" Nolan asked when they got to the living room.

"Oh, that's kind of you," she answered. "No, I don't mind at all. He'll be thrilled. But won't you be able to give it to him tomorrow yourself?"

"I'll be with my parents first thing, and after that I'm flying back to LA. There are some things I need to sort out."

Raina couldn't hold back the sound of dismay that escaped her. "Oh, I'd hoped…"

"I will return, Raina. I promise you that," he hastened to reassure her. "I'm taking the time now to pack up my apartment and settle a few matters before I move back here permanently. I'll be back for New Year's Eve."

She forced herself to smile. "I guess I'll have to be satisfied with that then."

He pressed a quick kiss to her lips. "I'll go get JJ's gift."

As Nolan went out to the car, Raina quickly retrieved JJ's gifts from where she'd hidden them in her room and put them under the tree. Once that was done, she sank down onto the sofa. She'd thought that life might get easier as she got older but it seemed that the complications only came in different forms. She had so much to consider. Did she, like JJ, love Nolan, too? The answer came back to her with resounding clarity. Yes, she did. Either way she turned it, it was clear to her that both she and her son had lost their hearts to the man who'd come into their lives so unexpectedly.

She heard Nolan come back into the house and stood as he entered the living room, an enormous wrapped parcel in his arms.

"Wow, that's huge. I hope you haven't gone to too much trouble," she said as she eyed the massive gift.

"No trouble at all. The first Christmas that I can remember, I was about JJ's age and got one of these. I always wanted to do the same for my—"

Raina frowned as his voice broke off. "For your…?"

she prompted. Maybe this would give him the opening to tell her everything.

"For another three-year-old," Nolan said on a rush of words. "It's a Spider-Man bike, with training wheels. It might still be a bit big for him but the seat and handle bars are adjustable and JJ's tall for his age. Anyway, I hope he likes it."

"He'll love it, but, Nolan, it's too much."

"No." He shook his head. "Where kids are concerned, it's never too much."

There was now a bleak note to his voice that Raina couldn't miss. She realized the holidays must be so hard for him and stepped forward to comfort him without giving it a second thought. Her arms slid around Nolan's waist and she reached up to kiss him gently on the lips.

"Thank you," she said simply. She studied him carefully, her eyes roaming his serious face with his beautiful brown eyes and straight blade of a nose. And those lips. She wanted to taste those lips again. She wanted… oh, she wanted so much more than that. "Will you stay with me tonight?"

Nolan's face grew even more serious than before. "Raina, I—" He shook his head. "I don't think that's a good idea just now."

"Please, Nolan. You could still stay with me a while tonight, couldn't you?"

Did she sound too needy? Too desperate? She hoped not. Raina held her breath, waiting for Nolan's reply.

"Yes, I'd like that."

"Then that makes two of us," she said with a slow smile spreading across her face.

Nolan kissed her. This kiss so different from the last. It was as if Nolan was trying to imprint himself on her, get lost in her, perhaps. Whatever it was, she welcomed him with equal fervor, her lips parting under his possession like the petals of a flower opening for the sun. Desire licked along her veins like wildfire and with it her body came to aching life.

Her breasts felt full and swollen in the cups of her bra, her nipples wildly sensitive against the lace. Nolan continued to kiss her like a man trying to lose himself in sensation, and Raina was only too willing to meet him head-on, matching his passion with her own.

She yanked his sweater up in the back and shoved her hands underneath, her palms flat on the warm smooth skin of his back. She stroked upward along the muscles that ran parallel to his spine then lightly scraped her nails down again. He shuddered in her arms, a groan coming from his mouth as he tore his lips from hers.

"Raina, I want you so much. I never thought I..." His voice trailed away and Raina pressed another kiss to his lips.

"Me either," she whispered softly against his mouth. "Make love with me, Nolan."

His pupils flared, making his eyes look darker, hungrier than she'd ever seen them. A shiver of need ran through her. Nolan was always so in control, so self-assured. She wanted to see him lose that control tonight, and she wanted to be the reason for it.

"Are you sure, Raina? There're things I haven't—"

Not tonight, not now, she decided. She didn't want another woman in bed with them tonight. Instead, she kissed him again. "I'm sure. I don't think I can say it any clearer than that."

A smile tugged at the corners of his beautiful lips. "I guess not," he agreed.

She shook her head and gave a small laugh. Even with her blood pumping through her body, her lips swollen from his kiss and her senses focused on the pleasure she knew she would attain with this man, he could make her laugh. It was a gift, she realized.

"Let's stop talking. Start doing," she urged, curling her fingers and embedding her nails in his back more firmly.

"Whatever the lady wants."

She led him to her bedroom where she gently closed the door behind them and flowed into his arms as if she belonged nowhere else in the world. And, right here, right now, she didn't.

His lips were teasingly gentle when they kissed this time. He made a sweet exploration of her mouth, her jaw, the sensitive cord of muscle down the side of her neck. She moaned as his lips burned a trail to the neckline of her blouse. He brought his hands up between them, his fingers busily plucking her buttons undone until he could ease the fabric aside. He pushed it off her shoulders and let her blouse drop to the bedroom floor.

Raina watched his face as he looked at her. The desire reflected there was tempered with a look of awe that made her feel invincible. As if his world, his attention, began and ended with her and no one else. This was what she'd always craved. A bond between two people that was so perfect that nothing could tear it apart.

Nolan eyes met hers and she quivered a little at the intensity of his gaze.

"I love you, Raina Patterson. I want you to know that before I show you just how much it's true."

She parted her lips to speak, but no words came out. Emotion closed her throat, making it impossible to speak, but he didn't appear to mind that at all as he slid his hands to her waist and skimmed them upward, his fingertips brushing her rib cage and sending goose bumps all over her skin.

He only took a second to size up the bed behind them. The double bed was small, but more than sufficient for their purposes, he thought as he backed Raina toward the mattress and guided her down onto it.

He eased himself over her body and, propping himself up with one elbow, began to trace featherlight designs on her skin with his fingertips, punctuating them with a kiss, a nibble, a swipe of his tongue. She quivered underneath his onslaught and he could see her pebbled nipples against the soft pink lace of her bra. He'd never been a big fan of pink, but right now it was most definitely his favorite color. Nolan bent to cover one tip with his mouth, sucking hard through the delicate lace. Raina's fingers threaded roughly through his hair and she held him to her. She arched her back, thrusting herself upward. Unabashedly offering herself to him.

Nolan released her nipple and traced the outline of her bra with his tongue. With his free hand he reached to cup her other breast before sliding his hand around to the back and unsnapping the fastening. The garment fell away from her body and he slowly guided the straps down her arms, taking his time, worshipping every inch of her as he did so. She shook beneath him as he paid homage to her beauty, to each scar he discovered, each stretch mark, every curve. When he got to her skirt, Raina lifted her hips so he could ease it from her and expose the delicate pink lace panties that matched the bra he'd already discarded somewhere on the floor.

Her body went rigid as he traced the edges of her panty line, his fingers lingering a moment in the hollow at the top of her thigh, eliciting a moan of delight from Raina. He bent closer to her, inhaling the musky sweet scent that was her signature, and nuzzled at her mound. He was rewarded with a gasp, her hands now at his shoulders, her fingers tightening until he could feel the imprint of her nails on his skin.

"I want to taste you, again," he murmured, nuzzling her.

"I'm yours," Raina replied, her voice strained and her body now as taut as a bow beneath him.

He whisked the last remaining barrier from her body and nestled lower between her legs, his fingers at the top of her thighs, pressing gently into her pale flesh and parting her legs that little bit more. When he sank down and teased her glistening flesh with a flick of his tongue, she moaned again—the sound almost enough to make him want to dispense with this foreplay and race straight to the main event. Inside his jeans his erection strained against the restriction of his clothing. He pressed his hips against the mattress in an attempt to relieve his body's demands but it was a short-lived respite.

To distract himself, he focused solely on the woman in his arms, intent on bringing her the kind of pleasure he dreamed of having the right to give her every day of her life. The taste and scent of her body filled him, exciting him to higher levels and driving him to see her every need fulfilled. He sensed that this—making love here in her bed—was the only time she wasn't holding back. Here in the sanctuary of her room, she was his alone and so he paid homage to the privilege she bestowed upon him. Loving her with every cell in his body until she arched beneath him, her body locked in paroxysms of pleasure before softening and sinking back down into the mattress.

Nolan swiftly stripped himself of his clothes and returned to her. His arousal demanded satisfaction but he waited until Raina's eyes cleared, until she was with him 100 percent.

"How do you do that?" she asked, sounding dazed.

"Give you pleasure, you mean?"

"Yes, that."

"I do it from my heart, Raina. I love you. It's that simple."

And with that, he eased his length within her, hissing a little between his teeth as her swollen wet sheath gripped him. It was almost more than he could stand but still he held himself in check. Raina's eyes were a glittering blue, punctuated by wildly dilated pupils. She met his gaze and reached for him, her hands gripping his hips and pulling him to her. He sank deeper into her body, deeper into pleasure, deeper into love, and with every stroke, every withdrawal, he affirmed that love until they both tumbled headlong into satisfaction.

Nolan watched Raina as she slept. They'd been about as close as two people could be. He didn't want to screw this up. It was too precious. Too important to him. He thought about the small package that was nestled at the bottom of his jacket pocket and the note he'd written to go with it.

The logical side of his brain told him that it was too soon to give it to her, but every other cell in his body told him to do it now. The thing was, he was ready—more than ready—to take the next step with her, to make her his forever. But was she? One word began to echo in the back of his mind. *Time.* He had to give her more time. And, he realized, he had to let her come to her decision at her own pace, without undue pressure from him.

Already he wished he didn't have to return to LA. There wouldn't be much to do. He'd barely existed when he'd lived there and he could tie up the loose ends within the week. Would a week be enough for Raina? Would it give her the time he felt she needed to be certain about them both and give them a chance to forge a future together? He certainly hoped so. And when he came back he needed to face his final demons. He needed to tell Raina about Carole and Bennett. He didn't want any secrets between them any longer. It had been one thing to convince himself that it was okay to hide his past, to bury it where it didn't hurt anymore, but Raina deserved to know everything and she deserved to know it from him.

Nolan eased from the bed and felt around in the dark for his clothes before slipping into the bathroom and quickly getting dressed. It was still pitch-dark outside and the sun wouldn't be up for at least another hour. Maybe it was wrong to be leaving her like this—letting her wake alone after all they'd shared together. But he also respected that she would need her space.

And then there was JJ to consider, as well. The little boy's Christmas wish had plucked at Nolan's heart and he'd wished he'd had the right to tell JJ that his wish could come true. He loved the child as if he was his own, there were no two ways about it. He wanted them both in his life but the decision lay firmly in Raina's gentle but capable hands.

Once he was dressed, Nolan walked through the house to the sitting room. The tree lights glittered with their myriad colors, making the small room look exotic and exciting. He knew it wouldn't be long before JJ wakened and raced to see what Santa had brought him. He wished he could be here to see JJ open his gifts, but with any luck he'd be able to share that delight with the little guy next year, and hopefully every year after that.

Nolan's heavy winter jacket lay over the back of an armchair where he'd discarded it last night. He reached into the pocket and pulled out the small gift and the envelope with the note he'd written for Raina before picking her and JJ up last night. He placed them under the tree, in among the gifts for JJ, then quietly let himself out of the house and into the burgeoning dawn.

Sixteen

"Santa's been here, Mommy. Wake up! Santa's been here!"

Raina opened one bleary eye then the other as JJ's joyful cries dragged her from sleep. She reached for Nolan, wondering how on earth they were going to explain his being there in bed with her, but her hand came up empty, the sheets cold beneath her touch. Raina quickly dragged on her nightgown and a robe and went to the living room where JJ was excitedly hopping from one foot to the other and staring at the bounty under the Christmas tree.

"Merry Christmas, JJ," she said, scooping her son up for a cuddle and a kiss. As she expected, he squirmed in her arms wanting to be put down to get to the serious business of opening gifts. "Remember the rules, JJ. Only one gift now. Granddad will be here to have breakfast with us and you can open all the rest then."

"Just one, Mommy?" JJ asked plaintively.

Raina held firm. She'd explained this all to JJ more than once in the days leading up to Christmas.

"How about you phone Granddad and let him know you're awake? He can let you know what time he'll be here."

JJ raced to do as she'd suggested, pressing the speed dial button on the phone Raina had taught him to use. After a brief conversation, he ran back to the Christmas tree. "Ten minnit!" he announced, hopping from one foot to the other.

"Great, now which gift are you going to open first?"

JJ zeroed in on the massive present Nolan had left under the tree for him. "This one," he said, and began tearing the paper off it immediately.

His squeal of delight was ear piercing when he saw the picture on the box. Raina hastened to help him open it and lift the bike out. There was a little assembly required but thankfully it only took a few minutes. Even better, Raina's dad arrived to do it all for her. He raised an eyebrow in her direction when he saw the bike, knowing it wasn't something she'd been able to afford for her son.

"It's from a friend, Dad," Raina said in explanation.

"Fancy wheels from a fancy man," he commented with a brusque nod, his eyes not budging from her face.

Raina felt the heat of a blush rise in her cheeks and she turned away from her father's piercing gaze.

"Now that you're here, I'll go and grab my shower and get dressed. Then I'll make us all breakfast, okay?"

Without waiting for a response, Raina flew down the hall toward the bathroom. She closed the door behind her and leaned against it for a few seconds, willing her blush to subside. Her father knew her too well. She'd seen that look on his face when she'd believed herself in love before. But this time it was different, she told herself. This time it was real.

Thankfully, her father didn't seem inclined to say any more on the subject, and after they'd had breakfast and opened all the presents under the tree, he went back to his place. Raina started to clean up the mess of wrapping paper and boxes that JJ had strewn all over the room in his exuberance. She'd hoped that he'd have happy memories of this day. Goodness knew she'd tried really hard to make it so. Right now, he was in his room, playing with some of his new toys until Raina could take him outside on the sidewalk with the new bike.

Raina almost missed the small parcel and envelope that had been placed at the tree's base. In fact it was already in her hand with the fistful of discarded paper when she felt it. After sorting through the paper and putting it in the trash bag, she sat down and looked at the items in her hand. Her pulse raced as she examined the small wrapped cube and the simple white envelope that accompanied it. Her name was written in bold black script across the front of the envelope and she traced the letters with a fingertip.

It wasn't her father's handwriting, which left only one other person who could have left it there—Nolan. Butterflies swarmed in her stomach, their tiny wings brushing against her nerves and making her hands tremble. What was this? Despite his words last night, could it be a farewell perhaps, or something else? There was only one way to find out but suddenly Raina found the prospect of reading whatever he had written more daunting than anything she'd ever done before.

Eventually she dragged in a deep breath and slid her finger under the flap of the envelope, tearing it open with a jagged edge. There was a single slip of paper inside, which she took out and unfolded.

Dear Raina,

I know we've only known one another a very short time, but believe me when I say that I'm very serious about wanting you in my life. I guess by now you've realized that I have something very special to ask you. I wanted to ask you last night, but I know you probably need more time to think about this and to be sure, so I'm giving you this next week—unencumbered by my presence—to consider what we mean to one another and particularly what I mean to you.

For my part, I know I don't want to spend the rest of my life without you by my side. I've learned, the hard way, that the special things in life can be torn from you at a moment's notice and that we need to reach out and grasp those gifts when we can—to cherish them and hold them dear to us, the way I want to cherish and hold you.

I only hope that you want the same as I do and that you'll let me be there with you and JJ, loving and supporting you both for as long as you'll let me. Nothing would give me greater pride or pleasure.

I'll be home on New Year's Eve and I'd be honored if you'd accompany me to the Texas Cattleman's Club function that night. You can give me your answer then. In the meantime, I would like you to open my Christmas gift to you and know that it comes from my heart and with my very best intentions.

All my love,
Nolan

Raina's fingers were wrapped tight around the small box in her hand, so tight that her knuckles whitened and her palms began to ache from the imprint of the edges of the box. Did he mean to ask her to marry him? Black spots began to swim in front of Raina's eyes and she realized she was holding her breath. She forced herself to breathe in and out, and again, until the spots receded.

Panic clawed at her throat. She'd thought she was ready for this but she so wasn't. They'd met less than four weeks ago. How could he be so certain she was what he wanted? How could she when she knew he still hadn't told her about the sadness of his past? There was still so much unsaid between them. The details of her past, of his. But did any of that matter when they loved each other?

Droplets of water dripped onto the sheet of paper in her hand and Raina realized she was weeping. The words on the paper blurred and she quickly refolded the sheet and shoved it back in the envelope. All the while, her heart urged her to take a risk on love again and her mind shrieked its horror in the background.

She'd taken risks on love before and she still bore the emotional scars from that. How on earth could she even contemplate marriage, if that was indeed what Nolan was suggesting, based on her track record with men? Hadn't it been a crazy, hormone-driven attraction that had seen her hook-up with Jeb in the first place? She'd been twenty-six, going on twenty-seven. Hardly a child by any means. She should have known better then—and she certainly knew better now.

Sure, deep down, she knew that Nolan was different from Jeb and the others she'd dated before him. But there was still that niggling sense of not knowing exactly where she stood with Nolan.

JJ would be thrilled at the chance to call Nolan Daddy. She knew that. But she had to be careful. She'd fought Jeb and beaten a tornado to give JJ a stable and secure home, a safe and happy childhood. She couldn't risk throwing that all away. Not now.

A voice in the back of her head reminded her that Nolan had acknowledged his initial deceit, that he'd apologized and done his best to make it up to her. That he'd even resigned from his job over it. Surely those were not the actions of a man who would stomp all over her heart and then walk away. He said he was back in Royal for good now. And she knew he meant it.

A kernel of hope began to bloom inside her until she reminded herself of the money that still sat in the safe back at Priceless and of the fact that Jeb probably still wanted it. While her ex certainly appeared to have dropped off the radar for now, who knew when he'd be back next or what his demands would be? How would Nolan react then? Would he be prepared to accept Raina with all her baggage?

"Mommy? Can we go outside now?"

JJ interrupted her jangled thoughts and Raina latched on to the chance to distract herself.

"Sure, honey," she said, shoving the envelope and the still-wrapped box in a drawer in the sideboard. She'd deal with it later. Maybe. "Let's get our coats on, okay?"

"Yippee!"

It was New Year's Eve and Raina was still in a quandary about Nolan's letter and the box that sat untouched in the drawer of her sideboard. She'd missed him this week. More because she'd known he was so far away. But he was back today and she'd alternately been filled with excitement and with a major case of the jitters.

"G'anddad's here!" JJ announced from where he'd been watching at the front window for his grandfather to pick him up and take him back to the trailer park to see in the New Year.

"Go and get your bag then, JJ," Raina suggested with a smile, turning away from the mirror where she'd been fussing with her hair for about the seventh time already that evening.

She went to the front door and opened it wide.

"You all right, girlie?" her dad asked, stomping his feet on the step before coming inside.

Raina welcomed her father with a huge hug and inhaled the special scents of his forbidden cigars and Old Spice.

"Yeah, Dad, I'm fine. Just glad to see you."

Her father gave her a sharp look and a small nod. "I heard some interesting news today. About your young man."

"My young…? You mean Nolan?"

"He's why I'm sitting for you tonight, isn't he?"

Raina felt the heat of a blush warm her cheeks and nodded. "Yes, he's taking me out tonight. What did you hear?"

Please don't let it be something bad, she wished with all her heart.

"Has to do with that no good piece of sh—"

"Dad! No swearing," Raina interrupted, glancing toward JJ.

"Well, you know who I mean."

"Jeb?"

"Who else?"

"What has Nolan got to do with Jeb?"

Her Dad gave her a sly smile. "Seems your young man arranged a meeting with the lowlife. Got him arrested and put away. Turns out he was wanted for third-degree felony over in New Mexico. Killed someone while driving under the influence and fled the scene, then jumped bail after that."

"But…how…when?" Raina was at a loss for words. How on earth would Nolan have known who Jeb was, let alone arranged for him to be arrested?

"Happened the night after the pageant, apparently. According to my poker buddy at the sheriff's office, Nolan offered him money to stay away from you, permanently. A goodly sum, so I'm told. That scumbag couldn't resist, of course, but it turns out he was dealing with the wrong person. Nolan apparently used his contacts to find out a bit more about who he was dealing with, and took his information to Sheriff Battle, who was only too pleased to oblige and take that waste of space off the streets. Apparently he put up a bit of a fight."

Did that explain the bruise on Nolan's face? Hard on the heels of that question came the realization that Jeb was in jail. Relief warred with confusion in Raina's mind.

"Anyways, doesn't sound like Jeb's going to be a problem for you again. You can thank your young man for that. I certainly plan to the next time I see him." Her dad fixed her with a steely look. "And I will see him a next time, won't I?"

"I… I don't know, Dad. I'm not sure I'm ready."

Her father harrumphed and pulled her into his arms for another hug. "You'll know when you're ready, my girlie. You'll know in your heart."

"But, Dad, we haven't known each other long en—"

"Time isn't what's important here. What you gotta ask yourself is what would your life be like without him in it."

Raina tipped her head to look up at her father. He'd had plenty of lady friends since her mom had left them, but never anyone who stuck around. "Is that what you asked yourself?"

He nodded. "I did, and I never got lucky enough to meet the lady I'd miss forever. Well, not yet anyway," he concluded with a twinkle in his blue eyes. "Now, where's that grandson of mine?"

After JJ and her dad had gone, Raina paced the living room floor, weighing her father's words and the news that Jeb was in jail. The relief she felt was slow to sink in, but bit by bit, the realization that she no longer had to worry about a random knock at her front door or being accosted on the street or receiving yet another late-night phone call or text began to seem real. A feeling of liberation filled her, a sense of freedom she hadn't known in a very long time—and she owed it all to Nolan.

What kind of man did what he'd done? A good man. An honest one. A man who was reliable and forthright and who looked after what was his to the very best of his ability and who wasn't afraid to ask for help when he couldn't do it alone. He'd protected her from harm, even when she hadn't asked for it. And she knew, deep in her heart, that Nolan would move mountains for her if she needed him to.

No matter which way she looked at it, Nolan Dane was a better person than she'd wanted to believe. She'd been so scarred by the actions of her past that she'd let them hold her back when she was being offered a chance to make a new start, a new beginning—filled with the kind of love she'd always dreamed of.

The sound of a car door slamming announced Nolan's arrival. Raina quickly grabbed the wrapped box from the drawer and slipped it into her evening purse.

He'd given her this week and she'd thought long and hard. And she'd reached her decision.

Seventeen

Nolan strode confidently up the path to the house and felt his heart lift when he saw the front door open to reveal Raina standing there, waiting for him. He'd missed her both physically and mentally. He'd lost track of the number of times he'd picked up the phone to call her, only to remind himself that he was giving her space to think.

Now the time had come for what he hoped would be the answer he'd been waiting for. Despite his eagerness, he wouldn't push. He understood her vulnerability, even though she projected such a staunch and strong face to the world. She needed to come to him on her own terms.

Framed in the doorway, she smiled nervously down at him. He bounded up the front steps to greet her the way he'd been waiting to do from the moment he'd left her bed, and she slid easily into his arms and lifted her face for his kiss. He kept it short and sweet, denying the nearly overwhelming urge he had to forget the night ahead and to simply sweep her off her feet, take her into her bedroom and pick up where they'd left off a week ago.

"I've missed you," he said simply, as he forced himself to release her.

She gave him a shy smile. "I've missed you, too."

"You look beautiful."

"Thank you."

Her cheeks flushed a delicate pink beneath the subtle makeup she wore and Nolan felt his heart squeeze in response. There was nothing he didn't love about her. He only hoped she'd let him tell her that every day now for the rest of their lives.

"You left without opening your Christmas gift," Raina said, reaching behind her to the hall table and passing a long slender parcel to him.

Nolan looked at it in surprise. This was the secret JJ had whispered to him about. "Can I open it now?"

"Sure," she teased, "unless you want to wait until next year."

He tore away the wrapping and instantly recognized the case he'd coveted a few weeks ago. He opened the lid and revealed the writing set inside. Nolan was staggered. Not just by the beauty of the gift, but by her thoughtfulness in giving it to him.

"It's old, of course," she said, sounding worried, "but in excellent condition. I remembered you looking at it and I thought—"

"I love it. Thank you, it's perfect."

He leaned forward to kiss her again. She was flushed when he finally let her go.

"Oh, you like it? Well…that's good then."

He smiled; she still sounded as if he'd knocked her off-kilter. She could barely meet his eyes as she reached into the cupboard behind her for her coat. He helped her into it, taking a moment to inhale the fresh herbal scent of her hair as she lifted it over her collar. He imagined his face buried in that sweet softness again and, as his body throbbed in response, was forced to turn his mind to other things.

"Shall we go?" Raina asked.

Surprised, because he'd hoped they'd talk about the gift he'd left for her before they headed out tonight, Nolan inclined his head. "My chariot awaits," he replied, gesturing for her to take his arm.

She locked the door behind her and they headed to the car where he stowed the writing set safely in the back. The journey to the Texas Cattleman's Club was conducted in silence, briefly punctuated by Raina asking how his trip to LA had gone. By the time Nolan handed his car keys to the valet outside the club, his stomach was a ball of nerves. Still not one word about his letter or his gift. He reminded himself that he was the one who'd set the parameters here. It had been his choice to leave her for this week and give her space and time to think about their future, if indeed they had one.

They circulated among the crowd, stopping and chatting here and there. The club was a large, rambling single-story building made of dark stone and wood that had originally been built in the early 1900s. The interior decor still reflected its Old World men's club heritage, with hunting trophies and historical artifacts adorning the paneled walls but, Nolan noticed, the ceiling had been lifted during the repairs after the tornado, giving the club an airier feel about it, and the colors were brighter and lighter than before. Overall the renovations better reflected the now mixed gender culture of what had long been solely a male domain.

In the great room, the mood was vibrant and celebratory, but Nolan knew he couldn't relax and celebrate until he had the answers he sought. During a lull in conversation with a group of his old high school buddies, Nolan tucked Raina closer to his side and drew her away to a quiet alcove he'd spied.

"Tired of the party already?" Raina teased.

Her cheeks were still softly flushed and her blue eyes sparkled, but he sensed that she was nervous. Possibly even as nervous as he was.

He smiled in response—it was now or never. "Actually, I was wondering what you thought of my Christmas gift."

The smile on Raina's face froze for a moment, before disappearing altogether and Nolan felt his hopes for the future slide inexorably out of his grasp. She reached into her small purse and pulled out the gift he'd left for her under the tree. His stomach dipped as he realized she hadn't even unwrapped it.

Raina looked up at him and he braced himself for the rejection he was sure was coming his way.

"I…" She stopped and chewed at her lower lip for a moment before continuing. "I didn't want to unwrap it without you there. You mentioned intentions in your letter. I need to know exactly what those are, Nolan."

It wasn't what he'd been expecting her to say and for a moment he was lost for words. But then the logical side of his brain kicked in and processed what she'd said. She wasn't rejecting him. She simply needed more reassurance. At least he hoped that's what was happening. He'd felt adrift like this once before in his life and he'd hated every second of it. It was why he'd been so reluctant to embrace the idea of sharing his life with anyone again. But he'd realized that he had to let himself be a little vulnerable if he wanted Raina to trust him. Trust him and love him.

"You know I love you, Raina, don't you?" he asked and felt a tentative swell of hope when she nodded. "I got off on the wrong foot with you to begin with and I can't apologize enough for that. The man I was then, the one who thought he could approach someone with an ulterior motive and damn the consequences—he's not the man I'm meant to be, nor the man I ever wanted to be. Do you believe me when I say that, too?"

Again she nodded and again he felt the tightness ease inside him that little bit more. Nolan led Raina over to a pair of chairs set against the wall in the alcove. They were surrounded by the noise and celebration of the crowd, and yet at the same time they were isolated. Locked in their own private space.

"I walked away from my life once," he began anew. "Things became more than I could bear and I had to leave or lose myself completely. I found a new way of living with myself. Unfortunately it didn't make me a very decent man.

"I like to think that everything in life eventually comes full circle and that fate took a hand in bringing me back to Royal. I wasn't ready to come back, I'll be honest with you about that. And I definitely wasn't ready to fall in love. But I did. Coming home has given me a new start—a chance to lead a good decent life again, a life I want to share with you and JJ, if you'll let me.

"I love you," he repeated and took both her hands in his, bringing them up to his lips to kiss her knuckles.

"I know you love me. I believe you, Nolan," Raina answered him quietly. "My father told me what you did with Jeb. Until I heard what he said and what you'd done, I think I was too afraid to trust my heart and let myself admit that I love you, too." She pressed one hand against his chest. "I know you have a good and decent heart, Nolan, and your actions have proved that to me when I wouldn't listen to what I really wanted to hear. You see, I don't have such a great track record with men. I don't tend to choose the stayers, or the reliable guys. In some ways I think I was just waiting for you to fail at the first hurdle because that would let me let you go."

"And I did fail. I failed you terribly."

"That's in the past, Nolan. You've more than made amends for that. You were acting for your client and, to be honest, even I can see now that you had no other option than to do the best for him at the time."

She looked up at him and Nolan saw tears swimming in her exquisite blue eyes. The sight made his heart wrench at the knowledge he'd put those tears there.

"Raina—" he started, but she put her fingertips to his lips.

"Shh, let me finish. You did what was right at the time, the same way you did what was right when you resigned your position with Samson Oil. I know that now." She took in a deep breath and her voice was so soft when she next spoke, Nolan could barely hear her. "I also know about Carole and Bennett."

The names struck him like a physical blow. "I planned to tell you, eventually," he said, his voice raspy with emotion. "It was more difficult than I thought."

"It's okay, Nolan. I understand that it's probably too painful for you to talk about them. For a while I've held that against you as another secret you were keeping from me. But I've let that go. Even so, there's still something that worries me. Something I need to ask you."

"Ask," he demanded.

"Do you love me and JJ because we remind you of your wife and son?"

Nolan felt her gaze lock on him with an intensity that showed him that everything now relied upon his response. He pushed aside the pain and the hurt, and chose his words carefully. His future happiness depended on how he said this.

"Raina, I will always love Carole and Bennett." His voice cracked on their names and he halted for a moment, closed his eyes and drew in a deep breath. "But they're gone. Losing them— I thought I'd never love again. That I never could. It wasn't just the pain of losing them, it was the risk of putting myself back out there again. Of maybe losing what little I had left of them, as well, if I let someone else into my heart.

"Meeting you has taught me that it's possible to love again without diminishing what I had with Carole, and trust me, I never thought I'd even want to feel about anyone the way I feel about you. You're so strong and so resilient. Life has battered you down and still you've shown your strengths by getting back up and moving forward. You haven't just been an example to me, you've opened my eyes to who I should be and shown me that I can loosen my grip on the past. Doing so allows me to think of a future. It's a future I want with you."

She nodded but remained silent. He looked down at the little packet in her hands.

"Will you open it now?" he asked.

His heart hammered in his chest. She could still return it to him. And he'd accept it and let her go if that was what she really wanted, even though the very thought threatened to tear his heart in two. He held his breath until she'd worked loose the tape that bound the wrapping, exposing the ring box. She lifted the lid and gasped. Inside, nestled against a dark velvet bed, lay his promise to her—a cushion-cut blue diamond edged with brilliant white diamonds and set in delicate platinum scrollwork.

Nolan dropped to one knee on the floor in front of her and lifted the ring from the box, offering it to her.

"Raina Patterson, will you do me the honor of becoming my wife? Will you let me be your husband for eternity and be a father to JJ and any other children we might be lucky enough to have?"

She appeared lost for words until he heard her choke on a sob. Tears rolled down her face but none of that mattered when he heard the words she was so desperately working to get out of her throat.

"Yes. Yes. Yes," she said repeatedly through her tears.

Nolan took her hand, slid the ring onto her finger and stood, pulling her to her feet. Raina lifted her face to his.

"I love you, Nolan. So very much. I was scared, I'll admit it. And probably too quick to look for reasons not to love you. I didn't want you to be able to hurt me and I didn't trust my own judgment anymore. But I do now. I love you and I'd be the happiest woman in the world to marry you. I'm so lucky to have you."

"I'm the lucky one, Raina. I never expected to be given another chance at love and life the way I have with you. And I want to spend the rest of my life showing you how much you mean to me."

He kissed her and, in her arms, found the sense of belonging that had been missing from his world for far too long. Her lips were sweet and tender and tasted of the promise of a future he never dreamed he'd want again. And yet, with Raina, he knew the future would be truly wonderful and that it was something he wanted to grasp with both hands and hold on to and cherish forever.

"They'll be doing the fireworks soon," he commented as they came up for air and he saw the crowd thinning in the great room as people started to move outdoors for the display. "Did you want to go outside to watch?"

Raina shook her head. "No, let's go home instead… and make our own."

* * * * *

MILLS & BOON®

Hardback – December 2015

ROMANCE

The Price of His Redemption	Carol Marinelli
Back in the Brazilian's Bed	Susan Stephens
The Innocent's Sinful Craving	Sara Craven
Brunetti's Secret Son	Maya Blake
Talos Claims His Virgin	Michelle Smart
Destined for the Desert King	Kate Walker
Ravensdale's Defiant Captive	Melanie Milburne
Caught in His Gilded World	Lucy Ellis
The Best Man & The Wedding Planner	Teresa Carpenter
Proposal at the Winter Ball	Jessica Gilmore
Bodyguard...to Bridegroom?	Nikki Logan
Christmas Kisses with Her Boss	Nina Milne
Playboy Doc's Mistletoe Kiss	Tina Beckett
Her Doctor's Christmas Proposal	Louisa George
From Christmas to Forever?	Marion Lennox
A Mummy to Make Christmas	Susanne Hampton
Miracle Under the Mistletoe	Jennifer Taylor
His Christmas Bride-to-Be	Abigail Gordon
Lone Star Holiday Proposal	Yvonne Lindsay
A Baby for the Boss	Maureen Child

1115 GEN STD HB

MILLS & BOON®

Large Print – December 2015

ROMANCE

The Greek Demands His Heir	Lynne Graham
The Sinner's Marriage Redemption	Annie West
His Sicilian Cinderella	Carol Marinelli
Captivated by the Greek	Julia James
The Perfect Cazorla Wife	Michelle Smart
Claimed for His Duty	Tara Pammi
The Marakaios Baby	Kate Hewitt
Return of the Italian Tycoon	Jennifer Faye
His Unforgettable Fiancée	Teresa Carpenter
Hired by the Brooding Billionaire	Kandy Shepherd
A Will, a Wish...a Proposal	Jessica Gilmore

HISTORICAL

Griffin Stone: Duke of Decadence	Carole Mortimer
Rake Most Likely to Thrill	Bronwyn Scott
Under a Desert Moon	Laura Martin
The Bootlegger's Daughter	Lauri Robinson
The Captain's Frozen Dream	Georgie Lee

MEDICAL

Midwife...to Mum!	Sue MacKay
His Best Friend's Baby	Susan Carlisle
Italian Surgeon to the Stars	Melanie Milburne
Her Greek Doctor's Proposal	Robin Gianna
New York Doc to Blushing Bride	Janice Lynn
Still Married to Her Ex!	Lucy Clark

MILLS & BOON®

Hardback – January 2016

ROMANCE

The Queen's New Year Secret	Maisey Yates
Wearing the De Angelis Ring	Cathy Williams
The Cost of the Forbidden	Carol Marinelli
Mistress of His Revenge	Chantelle Shaw
Theseus Discovers His Heir	Michelle Smart
The Marriage He Must Keep	Dani Collins
Awakening the Ravensdale Heiress	Melanie Milburne
New Year at the Boss's Bidding	Rachael Thomas
His Princess of Convenience	Rebecca Winters
Holiday with the Millionaire	Scarlet Wilson
The Husband She'd Never Met	Barbara Hannay
Unlocking Her Boss's Heart	Christy McKellen
A Daddy for Baby Zoe?	Fiona Lowe
A Love Against All Odds	Emily Forbes
Her Playboy's Proposal	Kate Hardy
One Night...with Her Boss	Annie O'Neil
A Mother for His Adopted Son	Lynne Marshall
A Kiss to Change Her Life	Karin Baine
Twin Heirs to His Throne	Olivia Gates
A Baby for the Boss	Maureen Child

1215 GEN STD HB

MILLS & BOON®

Large Print – January 2016

ROMANCE

The Greek Commands His Mistress	Lynne Graham
A Pawn in the Playboy's Game	Cathy Williams
Bound to the Warrior King	Maisey Yates
Her Nine Month Confession	Kim Lawrence
Traded to the Desert Sheikh	Caitlin Crews
A Bride Worth Millions	Chantelle Shaw
Vows of Revenge	Dani Collins
Reunited by a Baby Secret	Michelle Douglas
A Wedding for the Greek Tycoon	Rebecca Winters
Beauty & Her Billionaire Boss	Barbara Wallace
Newborn on Her Doorstep	Ellie Darkins

HISTORICAL

Marriage Made in Shame	Sophia James
Tarnished, Tempted and Tamed	Mary Brendan
Forbidden to the Duke	Liz Tyner
The Rebel Daughter	Lauri Robinson
Her Enemy Highlander	Nicole Locke

MEDICAL

Unlocking Her Surgeon's Heart	Fiona Lowe
Her Playboy's Secret	Tina Beckett
The Doctor She Left Behind	Scarlet Wilson
Taming Her Navy Doc	Amy Ruttan
A Promise...to a Proposal?	Kate Hardy
Her Family for Keeps	Molly Evans